Peter Gershkovich

ADAM EHRLICH SACHS

GRETEL AND THE GREAT WAR

Adam Ehrlich Sachs is the author of three books: *Gretel and the Great War*, *The Organs of Sense*, and *Inherited Disorders*. His fiction has appeared in *The New Yorker*, *n+1*, and *Harper's Magazine*, and he was a finalist for the Believer Book Award and the Sami Rohr Prize for Jewish Literature. He has received fellowships from the National Endowment for the Arts and the American Academy in Berlin. He lives in Pittsburgh, Pennsylvania.

GRETEL AND THE GREAT WAR

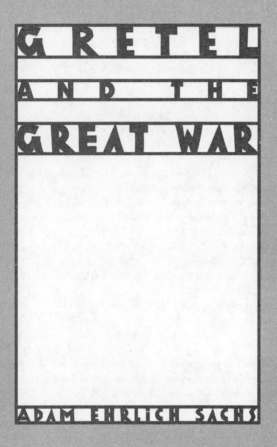

GRETEL

AND THE

GREAT WAR

ADAM EHRLICH SACHS

FSG ORIGINALS

FARRAR, STRAUS AND GIROUX

NEW YORK

FSG Originals
Farrar, Straus and Giroux
120 Broadway, New York 10271

Library of Congress Cataloging-in-Publication Data
Names: Sachs, Adam Ehrlich, author.
Title: Gretel and the Great War / Adam Ehrlich Sachs.
Description: First edition. | New York : FSG Originals / Farrar, Straus
    and Giroux, 2024.
Identifiers: LCCN 2023051867 | ISBN 9780374614249 (paperback)
Subjects: LCGFT: Novels.
Classification: LCC PS3619.A278 G74 2024 | DDC 813/.6—dc23/
    eng/20231106
LC record available at https://lccn.loc.gov/2023051867

Designed by Gretchen Achilles

Our books may be purchased in bulk for promotional, educational,
or business use. Please contact your local bookseller or the Macmillan Corporate
and Premium Sales Department at 1-800-221-7945, extension 5442,
or by email at MacmillanSpecialMarkets@macmillan.com.

www.fsgoriginals.com • www.fsgbooks.com
Follow us on social media at @fsgoriginals and @fsgbooks

1 3 5 7 9 10 8 6 4 2

For Tatyana

GRETEL AND THE GREAT WAR

n November 1919 a mute young woman was found wandering the streets of Vienna. She was handed over to the care of a neurologist, who wrote up her case in an issue of *Nervenkrankheiten*. No lesion, he concluded, could explain her condition, nothing organic, only a childhood deprived of language. Since she could not say who she was or what had happened to her, he welcomed correspondence from anyone with information about her past. He received a single response, from a patient at a Carinthian sanatorium who claimed to be her father. The girl's name, the man wrote, is Margarete—Gretel—and her childhood, whatever its privations, hardly lacked for language! Indeed, until his present confinement put an end to it, he used to tell her a bedtime story each and every night. He wrote now only to resume that cherished ritual. The doctor was asked to read her the enclosed story, titled A: THE ARCHITECT. She would understand it. The next day brought another story, B: THE BALLET MASTER, and the next day another, C: THE CHOIRMASTER, until there were twenty-six of them. Then they stopped, and the man wasn't heard from again. Whether the neurologist read her these stories, whether she understood them, whether she ever acquired the faculty of speech—not known. The letters were later sent on to Dr. Hans Prinzhorn, presumably in hopes of their inclusion in his celebrated collection of the art of the mad. Evidently Prinzhorn found them unsuitable; they turned up in his archives some eighty years later.

A

THE ARCHITECT OF ADVANCED AGE AT LAST BUILDS AN ABODE . . .

He is already old when he is hired to build his first building.

He is to build a new building for a high-end jeweler, with an atelier and apartments above it.

He declares that he intends to build a building far simpler than any building yet built. All buildings built to this point have been much too complicated. Even those buildings famous for their simplicity are too complicated, much too complicated!

Yet owing to the location of this particular building, on the same square as the Duke's residence, and facing the wing of the residence in which the youngest and most innocent of the Duke's seven daughters has her bedroom, the municipal authorities are reluctant to grant the architect permission to make the building as simple as he wishes.

To win their support, the architect proposes to lead the municipal authorities, as well as any interested members of the public, on a full-day architectural tour of the city in which he will point out only those buildings that have been built in a sufficiently simple manner, a manner befitting the function of a building as a dwelling place for man. By the end of the day it is observed that the architect has not pointed out a single building.

The architect offers this full-day architectural tour three days in a row. Never once does he point out a building.

This performance has the desired effect. The municipal authorities permit construction of the building to proceed. When it is finished, however, they determine that this building, which is even simpler than its blueprints had given them cause to imagine, is too simple, alarmingly simple, and that the completely unadorned facade, which the littlest Princess will inevitably gaze out on when she comes to her window each morning, poses a threat (the nature of which they are unable to articulate) to her innocence.

They therefore order the architect to adorn the bare facade.

He refuses.

Again and again they order him to adorn the bare facade, and again and again he refuses to adorn it. Their conflict comes to an end only with the architect's suggestion that he provide a daily adornment of the facade through the judicious use of flowerboxes, which he himself, by means of a hydraulic lift, will hang beneath every window at seven in the morning, before the Princess has risen, and remove again at nine at night, after she has gone to sleep. From nine at night to seven in the morning the building will assume its true form.

This compromise, which both safeguards the innocence of the little Princess and preserves the simplicity of the architect's building, manages to satisfy all parties, including the manufacturer of fine jewelry.

But the architect is cautioned that if, one morning, he neglects to hang the flowerboxes in time, or if, one night, he removes them too soon, and thereby allows the little Princess (who has never before laid eyes on a facade without an adornment of one kind or another) to glimpse the bare facade, the effect of which on such an innocent girl can only be imagined, the consequences for the architect's career, to say nothing of his building, will be severe.

His diligence in this matter proves to be beyond reproach. Early every morning and late into the night he can be found without fail on his hydraulic lift, hanging and unhanging flowerboxes. When the Princess flings open her curtains the facade that greets her is never anything less than conventionally adorned, and so it remains when she draws the curtains shut.

In time the architect develops a real affection for the Princess, an almost paternal affection, and he begins to take pleasure in the hanging of the flowerboxes, which he arranges with flowers specially calculated to win her approval, an approval she signals each morning with a bashful smile.

It cannot be denied that his flowers make her happy.

Long past the point in life when he believed himself capable of such transformations, he begins to reconsider his view of architecture.

One night, after he has removed the last flowerbox, he decides that when he hangs them again the next morning, he will screw them permanently in place.

But no sooner has he come to this decision than the light in the Princess's bedroom turns on. This is something that has never happened before. The architect thinks to himself: She has had a bad dream. He sees her shadow in the curtains. She is coming toward the window. She is going to open the curtains and look out. The architect does not have time to put the flowerboxes back on.

She is going to see the flowerboxless facade.

She is going to see the flowerboxless facade.

What will happen to the little Princess when she sees the flowerboxless facade?

Just as the Princess flings open the curtains, however, the architect is struck by the idea of turning his body into a spectacle. So the Princess scarcely notices the facade, all of her attention is drawn to the architect who's made a spectacle of his body. As a grown-up she will describe the moment she saw the architect on the hydraulic lift making a spectacle of his body in order to deflect her attention from the facade without flowerboxes as one of the two or three most formative moments of her childhood. When she draws the curtains shut again, the architect is certain that her innocence remains intact, and to protect himself from those architectural adversaries of his who will try to claim otherwise he publishes a precise account of what transpired that night. Whereupon he is committed to the Sanatorium Dr. Krakauer. From here he mails the municipal authorities a letter each morning informing them which combinations of flowers are likely to delight the Princess most.

The municipal authorities, who have the decency at least to execute his recommended floral arrangements, are unaware that by means of these ostensibly delightful arrangements the architect is in reality sending the little Princess messages containing information crucial to her continued survival in a city that is already much too complicated and which with every passing moment is only becoming ever more so . . .

Good night, my dear Gretel!

B

THE BALLET MASTER BURIES HIMSELF IN THE BAROQUE . . .

He uses his young daughter's wooden wagon to cart home from the Municipal Library book after book on the history of Baroque dance. Preclassical dance. His wife, who is also his principal dancer, is taken aback by the abuse he begins heaping on the art of classical ballet, to which until now they have jointly—and, she had thought, sincerely—devoted their lives. He informs her that the language of classical ballet, with all of its artifice, its five positions of the feet, is no longer sufficient for him, he can no longer express in it all that he needs to express, comments which seem calculated to wound her, for she is widely regarded as the world's greatest practitioner of classical ballet and her name is practically synonymous with that art.

To their young daughter the principal dancer poses questions the daughter is far too young to answer: What has happened to Papa? What does Papa mean by this? What does Papa seek in the Baroque?

When the principal dancer stands in the middle of the hallway and asks the ballet master in a theatrical manner whether she ought to feel ashamed that she has never felt the least bit constricted by classical ballet, not the least bit bored or deprived, he wheels a wagonful of books on Baroque dance in a wide arc around her body and replies, as he disappears into his office and locks the door, that that is a strange sort of question to ask. From inside his office he hears her emit a whimper just loud enough (and probably intentionally so) to wake their young daughter, who issues a piercing cry: *Mama!*

Eventually the ballet master exhausts the Municipal Library's ample holdings of books on Baroque dance and begins carting home books on the pre-Baroque, and then the pre-pre-Baroque, back toward the beginning of dance . . .

What does Papa expect to find in the pre-Baroque? In the pre-pre-Baroque? Questions the daughter is far too young to answer.

After a long period of immersion in these texts, the ballet master emerges from his office and announces that he has discovered a new position of the feet, a sixth position of the feet, a far more natural position of the feet, probably the most natural possible position of the feet, a foot position in perfect harmony with the needs and the nature of the human body.

The principal dancer, however, is unable to put her feet in this position without immediately falling over.

It does not escape the ballet master that the—ostensible—inability of his wife, the most technically skilled ballerina in Europe, to stand in this perfectly simple, perfectly natural position is the means by which she can express her anxiety about his artistic trajectory, which seems to be bending away from her; she suspects that when he choreographs now he pictures in his mind a different body than he did before, and in a way she is not wrong; but she does not dare say any of this aloud, only by means of these expertly contrived falls; and so, in the face of her falling, her constant simulated falling, he displays a forbearance uncharacteristic of him, and restricts himself to informing her with a low bow that he has already begun choreographing a full-length ballet in which the foot position in question is to play a central part.

He promptly completes this ballet, well before his wife has mastered the ability to stand in the position.

The ballet requires her to stand in the position almost uninterruptedly for about three hours. Every step begins in the position, every step ends in the position. In this movement from the position to the position, every step passes through the position. For three hours, the position. The ballet is to be performed without intermission.

She begs him to postpone the premiere of the ballet until such time as she is able to stand in the required position without falling over.

He knows, but does not say, that when she is actually performing before her legions of fans, who number among them the Duke himself and his dance-crazy daughters, she will be able to stand in the position without the slightest difficulty. It is a position anyone can stand in, because it is the position we were meant to stand in, and once stood in, before we began to scrutinize how we stand. But he does not say this. He merely replies that for logistical reasons the premiere of the ballet cannot be postponed.

She whispers something into the ear of their young daughter. He watches her whisper it, and she watches him watch her, and he can't help but notice that as she watches him watch her whisper it, her eyes gleam insanely. Later, when he presses his daughter to tell him what Mama said, she says Mama said that there is nothing natural about Papa's foot position! That Papa spent more than two years alone in his office coming up with a crazy way to position the feet! A really crazy way to position the feet! That something strange is happening to Papa! That we must keep our eyes on Papa! That Mama feels sorry for Papa but she is also afraid of Papa! That Papa's foot position is not at all natural! That *the feet don't go that way*! That Papa wants to make a fool of Mama and has figured out how to do so! But that if Mama falls onstage it will make a fool of Papa too!

The mental state of the principal dancer begins to concern the ballet master. But at the same time it enrages him that in what is fundamentally an aesthetic struggle, between her commitment to the stylized and the artificial and his own exploration of the ever more natural, the principal dancer would enlist their daughter, who is far too young to understand the aesthetic nature of it and must therefore interpret it in a more personal way. Indeed, his daughter, who he suddenly notices has been dressed in a smaller version of the principal dancer's own elaborately filigreed outfit, now flinches in fear of him. He returns to her her wooden wagon, with admiring words for its simple, sturdy construction ("Humanity has not yet improved upon the wagon!"), but this does nothing to repair their relationship. He suppresses his anger long enough to reiterate to his wife that the premiere of the ballet will take place as scheduled.

In the days before the premiere the ballet master and the principal dancer regard each other with hatred, fear, and disgust.

The night of the premiere arrives.

The curtain rises at the City Theater.

The principal dancer emerges from the wings to clamorous applause, performs a series of pirouettes toward the lip of the stage, comes to a halt there in the new position of the feet, and plummets headfirst into the orchestra pit, producing, from the collision of her skull with the edge of a kettledrum, a sound that the audience construes as comic, until a piercing cry of *Mama!* silences their laughter.

The principal dancer is brought home to the family villa. Now and then her limbs flail in a disturbing fashion, but a physician declares that in the technical sense of the term she is no longer alive. The ballet master deems it in his daughter's best interest not to see her mother in this state. The next morning he notifies the journalists and balletomanes gathered on the lawn, including the sobbing Duke and his seven somber daughters, that the principal dancer has died. That is how her own daughter learns of it. But she is far too young to know what it means. The questions she poses indicate beyond any doubt that she does not know what it means to die. Nor does she stop demanding to see her mother, until finally the ballet master—who can no longer ignore, as he observes the affected way she prances about and positions her feet, in her finely filigreed outfit, that his daughter, as young as she is, has already been claimed by classical ballet—ships her off to the Imperial Ballet School in St. Petersburg.

Then in the family villa it is once again just the ballet master and the principal dancer. For as it turns out, she isn't dead. The physician got it wrong. The fact is, doctors don't know anything about movement. They always get it wrong when they try to deduce something about our minds from our movements. No one knows anything about movement, *everyone knows everything about the mind*, no one knows anything about movement. It turns out she's not dead. As a matter of fact, she hasn't moved so expressively in quite a long time. Probably since before her most advanced ballet classes. These advanced ballet classes, he tells her, stroking her face, these advanced classes that did so much harm: these advanced ballet classes have been effectively undone.

Her feet, he notices, are in sixth position.

He is pleased to point this out to her.

Now he can teach her to dance.

THE CHOIRMASTER CAN FEEL THE CONGREGATION'S CONTEMPT AS HE CONDUCTS THE CANONICAL COMPOSER'S CANTATA . . .

Their eyes bore into his back because he cannot coax from the throats of his boys as pure a sound as the great composer once coaxed from them.

What he coaxes from the throat of Hillmeyer, alto soloist, is, in particular, less pure than it ought to be.

He tries in his classes to work on the boys' voices, but the boys are rambunctious, he can hardly control them, there is little improvement.

The rector of the boarding school, who along with the choirmaster is responsible for the welfare of its fifty-five choirboys, a responsibility that in light of their rambunctiousness has aged him prematurely, does his best to reassure his colleague. The eyes of the parishioners are on his back only because the conductor's back is a natural focal point for their gaze; and since no one can possibly know how the choir sounded a century ago, under the direction of the canonical composer, no one is drawing any unfavorable comparisons.

The choirmaster is reassured. It is only in his own head that comparisons are being drawn to the purity of the sound elicited by the composer. For the first time he takes pleasure in his position. The quality of the boys' singing, even Hillmeyer's singing, pleases him, it is pure enough, and their rambunctiousness, even Hillmeyer's rambunctiousness, delights him. He hears himself saying to the rector: When you have tired of the rambunctiousness of boys, you've tired of life itself! Yes, he loves the boys, the fifty-five boys. The choirmaster proposes a toast: To the rambunctiousness of the boys!

The next Sunday, however, as his choir sings another cantata, he feels the congregation's eyes again boring into his back, a feeling that does not go away even after the church has cleared out. It can no longer be doubted that a trace of a memory of the canonical composer's sound has indeed been preserved in the collective consciousness of the city.

Then the choirmaster realizes that the church has not cleared out completely.

There is still an old woman in the third pew.

The old woman speaks.

As a preliminary matter she wishes to inform the choirmaster that she has reached an age greater than the human organism typically allows one to reach. Her quest for justice has enabled her to surpass certain unsurpassable biological limits. She is simply stating this as a fact, she is not asking the choirmaster to believe her, the choirmaster's belief doesn't matter to her in the least. Her father had had a big mill deep in the woods. Yes, deep in the woods, she is not asking the choirmaster to believe her! In this big mill bad things had taken place. All the more so after her mother died.

Mother had always been sickly and weak and had been hated by her children for not stopping these bad things from happening. Yet she must have stopped some of them because when she died the number of them increased. While Father did these bad things he sang songs in a beautiful baritone. The singing you would have heard had you passed by their mill would have given you the wrong impression of what was happening in it. There was a time when she thought that all fathers did such things but only hers sang so beautifully. Only later did she realize that the things he did were as uncommon as the voice he had. Now, it was not only to her that he did these things, he did them to her six older brothers as well. And it happens that all seven of them inherited his beautiful voice. So Father put them into this predicament but furnished them also with the means to escape from it. Or at least furnished his six sons. For when each son reached a certain age he auditioned before the great composer and ascended into the choir loft. The very loft where the choirmaster now stands. She was happy for her brothers. But as each of them escaped into the boys' choir, the predicament, which had been borne by all seven of them, and therefore divided by seven, was borne by six, and then by five, then by four, three, two, until it was borne by her alone, divided by one. As soon as she came of age she pinned up her hair with one of her dead mother's hairpins, put on one of her father's hats, and presented herself before the great composer. She only knew Father's favorite songs, so it was one of those that she sang. When she finished singing the composer clapped enthusiastically but also reached under her hat and removed the pin. Her long hair came tumbling down. She had to go back to the big mill in the woods. For eleven more years. Eleven more years, she is not asking the choirmaster to believe her. But before returning to the mill she received the composer's permission to ask him a question. There was one question she'd always wanted to ask him. How do you coax such a pure sound from the throats of your boys? The composer smiled, looked to his left, looked to his right, and whispered: The trachea of a boy is no different from the pipe of an organ, except that a boy's trachea has at the base of it a small protuberance. This protuberance must be removed.

With that the old woman rises and leaves the church.

The choirmaster laughs loudly and prolongedly in the empty church to prove to God and himself that he has not taken seriously anything the old woman told him.

Yet at the first opportunity he finds himself peering deep into Hillmeyer's throat with a terrifically powerful electric flashlight.

And he is astonished to see at the base of his throat the very protuberance of which the old woman spoke.

On the one hand he is happy to see the protuberance, because the protuberance explains everything. On the other hand he is frightened to see it. He clicks the flashlight off and banishes the protuberance from his thoughts. He banishes from his thoughts the notion of a perfectly pure cantata. Yet the small protuberance and the notion of a perfectly pure cantata cannot stay out of his thoughts for long. He knows that the protuberance in the end will have to be dealt with. The first seven surgeons the choirmaster approaches are, however, incapable of seeing the protuberance. Not because it is too small. They do not see the protuberance because they do not want to see it. It is easier not to see it. But the eighth surgeon, a specialist in the ear, nose, and throat, albeit of animals, is able to see the protuberance, willing to see the protuberance. The operation is conducted in the choirmaster's own quarters, while the rector knocks first tentatively, then emphatically, and finally frantically on the door. Owing to Hillmeyer's remarkable rambunctiousness, a double dose of ether is needed. The rector later testifies that among the many terrible sounds coming out of that room, he thinks he heard someone singing. The choirmaster, who is ultimately committed to the Sanatorium Dr. Krakauer, testifies that the person the rector heard singing, and singing so well, was Hillmeyer himself.

And you, Gretel: Do you still like to sing? Perhaps you're too shy around your doctor? But with me you sang so beautifully, otherwise our little lodgings would've been very quiet indeed! In fact I always thought it was you, not your mother, who could carry a tune! Good night!

THE DUCHESS IS DIVIDED . . .

Her ladies-in-waiting lace her corset as tight as they possibly can, in order to make the body of the Duchess appear smaller than it is.

Once she truly was slender. Then her seven daughters came along. When they were little it seemed worth it, because they loved her. But now they're all big and want nothing more to do with her.

All except the seventh. Yes, the seventh one is still little. She still needs her Mama, she still thinks she's pretty!

She loves nothing so much as to watch Mama get dressed, and most of all the lacing of her corset.

Inasmuch as she is very strong, stronger than a lot of grown-ups even, she can probably lace Mama the tightest of anyone!

The ladies-in-waiting hand over the laces. The consequences of this, however, are catastrophic. For owing to the little girl's fantabulous strength the Duchess first grows short of breath, then can speak only in whispers, and finally—

Oh, dear.

What is it, Mama?

No, no, this is not comme il faut . . .

What happened?!

What's happened is that the Duchess has been split in two at the waist!

The little Princess giggles. She knows that Mama must be tricking her. Because a person can't really be cut in half like that, not without a sword. Right?

You're tricking me, Mama!

Yet the sustained nature of Mama's anguish, her desperate efforts to hold the two pieces of herself together with her hands, how she has to stand straight and still as a pole to balance the one on the other: All of this means it can't be a trick. Because if it were a trick none of this would be necessary, and it would've stopped by now, it wouldn't still be going. So it isn't a trick, her Mama's actually in two pieces, a top and a bottom!

Suddenly Mama falls silent and topples over onto the bed.

Her ladies-in-waiting, who have always despised Mama despite how good she is to them, grin a little, because they are so happy Mama is dead.

But the little girl bursts into tears, climbs onto the bed, and buries her face in Mama's lap.

And good thing, too: Her loving tears seep under Mama's clothing and not only bring her back to life but also cause her bottom and her top to stick back together. Her love is the glue that makes Mama whole again! In fact she is the only one of the seven daughters who loves her. And she promises never to get any bigger, right? The way her six big sisters did? She'll stay little and loving forever and ever?

Yes, Mama!

As proof of that she has the little Princess brought to her every morning; has her lace up her corset; is divided in two by her fantabulous strength; and knows from the little girl's giggles and then from her tears that she has not yet grown up.

And she never will?

No, Mama!

The way her six sisters did?

Not me, Mama, I promise!

But the Duchess doesn't believe her, because grow up is what little girls do. She has seen it happen six times before. First they need their mother for everything. Then for less and less. Finally they don't need her for anything at all. Then they begin to roll their eyes at the mother and prefer the company of the father. Everything the mother does irritates them, it is embarrassing and old-fashioned, it is mad, she is mad, they must call Dr. Krakauer. She has seen it happen six times before.

However, it is not in the *nature* of a little girl to grow up. Left to her own devices she would not know to do so. What makes her grow up is the outside world. So commerce between the world and the Princess is kept to a minimum. She must content herself with seeing it through the window of her bedroom.

One night—

(But of course this part, my dear Gretel, you already know!)

One night she sees something through the window, on the un-adorned facade of the facing building, that makes her grow up lickety-split.

The next morning, as she laces the corset, there are neither giggles nor tears. Mama, please, I don't want to play this game anymore.

And she laces it so tight that for the first time the ladies-in-waiting need not redo it when the Princess leaves the room.

Now it is the Duchess who bursts into tears. She feels faint. Her ladies-in-waiting help her lie down. When next she opens her eyes she sees that it is dark, and that her legs are gone. So, she must be dreaming. Curious nevertheless to know where her legs are, the top part of her hoists itself off the bed and maneuvers down the hallway. Her legs at first are nowhere to be found. Then she finds them with her daughter, amongst the dolls and stuffed animals invited to share her bed tonight, the largest of them, and, to judge by the way the sleeping child has entwined herself around them, tonight's favorite. The Duchess grabs hold of her legs in order to reattach them. But her legs want nothing to do with the rest of her.

They wriggle free and dash off. Her top part pursues them. The legs naturally have the advantage of speed. But the torso and head have the advantage of sight. So long as they remain at home, or within the well-lit confines of the city, the top succeeds in gaining on the bottom. When, however, they reach the ducal game preserve, her legs slip between the trees and are gone. A moment later she hears a rifle shot, and then one more, which is strange inasmuch as hunting is forbidden in that forest. But of course in a dream, the Duchess knows, strange things can happen. Then the top of her returns to the city and hoists itself back into bed, and when she opens her eyes again her legs and torso are rejoined at the waist.

So, yes: A dream. With all the hallmarks of a dream.

But when she sits up in bed and swings her legs over the side, her ladies-in-waiting gasp, because her bare legs are covered in scratches and scrapes. Their provenance is obscure to them. But the Duchess knows these are exactly the sort of scratches and scrapes one would suffer in the woods.

Trembling, she proceeds to the bedroom of her littlest one, shakes her awake, and poses the simple question of whether or not her legs slept there last night. But the drowsy child can't possibly understand that this one simple question will decisively demarcate dream from reality. She regards it rather as the labored continuation of a game she has already long since outgrown, and therefore replies to it with a roll of the eyes. Only her mother's reaction to that brings home the true seriousness of the matter, and sends her scurrying for her father.

By the time the Duchess returns to her room Dr. Krakauer is already there waiting for her. He looks up and down at her corpulent figure and says what he always says: Her Grace has to eat something, she is wasting away . . .

So, her little one really is all grown up! To the point even of summoning doctors! She's really no different from the others now. Now the Duchess needs another one. Now she needs a little boy.

E

THE EXPLORER EXISTS IN HIS ENTIRETY ONLY ON ENTER-
ING THE EMPTY PLACES OF THE EARTH . . .

Every day he lingers in this city, this contrived, hypocritical,
highly populated city, is one more day on which he doesn't really
exist. Here, in the city, he explains, he is dead. Only in the Earth's
remaining void spaces, the places where men do not and cannot
live, not for long, is he alive. It is for this reason that the explorer
goes from patron to patron of a certain fashionable coffeehouse
in search of a soul capable of joining him on an expedition to just
such a void space.

The man who will join him must have four qualities rarely to be
found in one person. First, he must possess a spirit of irrepress-
ible optimism. Second, an interest in birds. Third, the ability to
haul a 150-kilogram sled across ice without slipping. And fourth,
no family attachments.

This fourth point is important, the explorer always informs the
patrons of the coffeehouse. Suppose you possess a spirit of ir-
repressible optimism and an interest in birds, and are capable
of hauling a 150-kilogram sled across ice without slipping, but
you have family attachments. Do you suppose that I can take you
with me?

No, replies the coffeehouse patron.

No! cries the explorer. You are correct, sir, I cannot! Not with family attachments! Not even if you have the optimism, the interest in birds, and the ability to haul the sled! I shall explain why.

Now the explorer, who to this point has remained standing, suddenly sits down at the patron's table and tells his tale:

Once, when he embarked on an expedition to one of the Earth's northernmost void spaces, he left his young daughter in the care of a French governess who came with impeccable credentials and was in every way ideal except that it struck him as a little strange that she wore in her hair two red ribbons, for which the governess was (or so the explorer thought, though he acknowledged even as he was thinking it that the thought was a petty and probably unfair one) slightly too old . . .

Here the explorer always interrupts himself with a violent shake of his head. No, no, if I am to tell the tale properly, I must begin further back! . . . And Gretel, I'm simply telling it to you the way the explorer always tells it to the patrons of this coffeehouse! You may, by the way, start to wonder: In a city famously filled with coffeehouses, why do these patrons still willingly go to this particular coffeehouse, where the explorer always lies in wait for them? And why does the proprietor of the coffeehouse allow him on the premises? That, too, my dear, is something I can clear up, but only at the end, before I kiss you good night. And perhaps by then you'll be in a position to guess!

The explorer begins again further back:

Long before his expedition to the northern void space there had been an expedition to a certain void space in the south . . .

But this southern void space, it turns out, was not completely void. There was a people there. At first these people drove him from their presence. Soon, however, he won their trust and, by relating their utterances to their actions as they uttered them, mastered their tongue. He also shot a number of birds. A successful expedition. But he returned home with a mysterious illness no one at the Pathological-Anatomical Institute had ever seen before or expected him to survive. A very distinguished physician declared that in the technical sense he was already dead.

A quarantine was established, such that his wife and daughter had to communicate their farewells through an extraordinarily thick pane of glass.

But it was obvious from the joyous way she thumped on the thick glass that the little girl did not grasp that in so doing she was saying goodbye to her father.

His wife found this misunderstanding so heartbreaking that she flouted the injunction of the distinguished physician by rushing into the quarantine area to embrace her husband.

From that point on he began, miraculously, to improve. She, however, contracted from him the mysterious illness and in short order was dying of it.

Now, the wife, in contrast to the explorer, was by nature a homebody, and considered the world beyond the city a malevolent entity, not merely an indifferent one, with especially wicked intentions for their daughter. It was her unwavering conviction that every stranger who smiled at the little girl wanted to snatch her and every food item that provoked the girl's desire was far too large for her gullet. From the day of her birth she had never let her out of her sight. The explorer had never succeeded in persuading his wife that she was, in this respect, a paranoiac. Even her three-day stay at the Sanatorium Dr. Krakauer, to which she agreed to go only on the condition that she could bring her daughter with her, was no help, for afterward she told the explorer that Dr. Krakauer had told her that her fears in fact were well-founded. The girl was of course much too young to corroborate or contradict her mother's claim, and Dr. Krakauer, when consulted directly, inevitably cited patient confidentiality.

Therefore his wife's dying wish came as no surprise to the explorer: That he not let their daughter out of his sight. That he not set foot outside the city again until she was big enough to fend for herself. Promise!

What could he do? What could he do? He promised.

What if, she said (and these, the explorer always tells the coffeehouse patron, were her last words), he came to find their daughter as fascinating as he found the world, such that staying put was no sacrifice?

But it was not so: He found the world more fascinating. Again and again he compared his daughter to the whole of the outside world, the world beyond the city, and again and again his daughter suffered by comparison. It was not her fault. *Verum ipsum factum!* We know what we have made! He had made her, so he knew her! Man had made the city, so man understood the city! Whereas nature . . . the void spaces . . .

He brought his daughter as far as the city limits and, gazing out past them into the woods, wondered how long it would be until she was big enough to fend for herself. Fend for yourself, what does that even *mean?* he asked her, as with a toe of his heavy-duty explorer's boot he nudged one pebble and then another across the line of the city limits, until he'd caused a whole grouping of small pebbles to be moved from within the city to beyond it. He spat across the city limits and wondered whether by doing so he had broken his promise to his wife. Does anyone apart from an outlaw truly fend for themselves? he thought as he very slowly extended both of his arms across the invisible plane stretching upward into the heavens from the line of the city limits.

First uncertainly and then more and more forcefully and with increasing self-possession he thrust the crown of his head repeatedly through this invisible plane.

Now it seemed clear that he had broken his promise. His lower limbs were still within the city limits but with his whole head outside them and both arms also it seemed clear that the spirit of the promise had been violated. *This* couldn't be what she had had in mind. The promise was broken. His mind had departed from the municipality. He laughed. His daughter laughed, too. She was laughing because he was laughing. He was laughing at the feebleness of the force that hitherto had kept him confined to the city. He now stepped across the city limits with inconceivable ease.

He hired the French governess. She untied one of the red ribbons from her hair, knelt beside the explorer's daughter, and tied it around the daughter's wrist. The daughter's affection was thereby won. So that's what the red ribbons are for! the explorer thought. But it explained only one of the ribbons, not the other one.

Holding the hand of the governess, the daughter issued no complaint as the father embarked on an expedition to the Earth's northernmost void space.

He climbed up and down a steep mountain.

Navigated a vast and treacherous waterway.

Hauled a 150-kilogram sled across ice so thick and clear that when he glanced down expecting to see his own reflection he saw instead with appalling precision the lifeless bed of a fathomless lake.

He thought: This was actually in her best interest, for if I had stayed in the city even one day longer I would have become unaccountable to myself.

And he came to the point where, in the old chronicles, the void space began.

Now, though, there was a people there.

He tried to win their trust and master their tongue, but felt he was failing to understand them inasmuch as they spoke continually of ribbons, an object they did not possess and on which they had never laid eyes and which, therefore, was an unlikely candidate to be a cornerstone of their language. When he related their utterances to their actions, the evidence indicated that they were speaking continually about ribbons. But when he reflected on whether this was logically possible, or anthropologically plausible, he had to admit it was not. When he showed them a sketch of a ribbon, they did not react, and when he kept showing them this ribbon sketch they never reacted, so he had to conclude that the word they were uttering meant something other than ribbon. In the end the people drove him from their presence.

The explorer continued north, but before reaching the start of the void space he came to another people, who spoke of nothing but governesses, French governesses. It beggared belief, however, that a concept like that would be so central to a people like this. He must have been misunderstanding them.

The third people he came to uttered only the sentence *The French governess uses the red ribbon to asphyxiate the little girl!* This, too, was obviously a mistranslation.

Yet this mistranslated sentence sounded continuously in his head as he climbed the final ridge that stood between him and the void space. Just before he crested the ridge and set eyes on the void space, and the rare and beautiful birds that no doubt lived there, the sentence *The French governess uses the red ribbon to asphyxiate the little girl!* became, at last, too much for him. Three steps before cresting the ridge the explorer turned around and hurried back to the city as fast as he could.

Here the explorer falls silent.

After a moment, as delicately as he can, the patron says: And ... ?

And what?

And . . . was your daughter . . . ?

The daughter's not the point! The turning back is the point! The turning back is the point! No family attachments! the explorer cries, adding: You, sir, strike me as the ideal candidate to join me on my expedition into one of the last remaining void spaces on Earth. I depart on the eleventh. Will you join me?

The patron agrees, they shake hands, and the explorer—whom, incidentally, no one can recall ever leaving the city, not once, not even in his youth—shuffles off to the next table, the next candidate . . .

Now then, Gretel, the question remains: Why does the proprietor allow such a person in his coffeehouse? Why do the patrons still patronize it? Have you figured it out? The answer is: *This coffeehouse is patronized mainly by members of a circle of poets and pseudo-revolutionaries whose aesthetic theories have led them to romanticize and mimic in their work the symptomology of certain psychoses that they consider characteristic of city living, such that the "explorer" has become for them a model, mascot, and source of creative inspiration, to the point that many of them can't even start writing for the day until the "explorer" has invited them on one of his expeditions to a void space, and they have accepted, even though they've all been invited a million times already! And therefore the proprietor has been repeatedly petitioned by his own clientele not to kick the "explorer" out, much as he might like to!*

See, for example, how the very patron whom the explorer has just been addressing, a neurologist with philosophical pretensions, who beforehand was staring off into space, probably convinced he had nothing original left to say, that he might as well do away with himself, now delves straight into a piece of writing! Straight into a short essay on language, meaning, ethics, and modernity!

I kiss you good night!

F

THE FATHER, A FORMER PHYSIOLOGIST, FINDS FELLOW FEELING—IF ONLY FLEETINGLY—WITH THE FORMER PHYSICIST . . .

Father Franz occupies the room beside mine.

He has been diagnosed with narcissism, catatonia, and moral insanity.

I believe his diagnosis is correct, because, for example, as I know from listening through the wall we share, he cannot be swayed from his conviction that at the end of the day he will be compelled by Dr. Krakauer, acting as an agent of God, to ingest all of the waste of the world, for his sins.

If Dr. Krakauer has evidence to the contrary, evidence, in other words, that Father Franz will *not* be forced at the end of the day to ingest the world's waste material, Dr. Krakauer is invited to put it forward, by all means! But of course Dr. Krakauer does not know what such evidence would even look like, an admission that Father Franz receives with satisfaction.

He can be brought to acknowledge that yesterday did not end that way, nor the day before, nor the day before that. But this, to him, is no proof of anything, it only goes to show that "today's the day."

In light of this belief, which he knows to be irrational, even mad, but is no less true for that, nothing he does here (in the world) matters, "all of it will anyway be ingested" by him. Every action taken, every thought expressed, only adds to the world's waste, with the consequence that the sum total of what he will have to ingest at the end of the day increases. Why start something if he will only end up ingesting it. Hence his catatonia.

Now, Gretel, will you believe that early this morning, this catatonic man, whom I have never before seen out of bed, knocks on my door, bounds into my room, brushes aside all questions about the change in his mood, and with considerable urgency, but also a twinkle in his eye, tells me the following story? The story of how he, Father Franz, formerly a godless student of physiology, found religion?

In his youth he was part of a circle of physiology students whose ambition was to renew language by removing its encrustations and digging up everything dead and redundant in it, whatever sagged or had no meaning anymore, and then redraping what remained over the structure of reality and pulling it as taut as possible. Whatever was left over after this highly scientific reupholstering was also to be cut off and discarded. All this was done to language at a certain coffeehouse near the Pathological-Anatomical Institute. Across the street stood a Cistercian monastery, the oldest in the city. Needless to say, the students regarded monasteries as manufactories of linguistic mystification. It was helpful to keep the monastery in view as a constant reminder of what happens to language when it retreats into a sanctuary and renounces its duty to the world. The duty to describe the world as it is. After one meeting, in which language was critiqued and considerably clarified, though in the process at least one piece was dug up and discarded that Franz wasn't convinced was dead, the students, too exhilarated by the purification of language to go straight home, had the idea of attending vespers at the monastery and then tormenting the monks by innocently inquiring as to the meaning of the word *grace* and querying in turn every word given in definition until the groundlessness and emptiness of their whole way of speaking and thinking became clear to them. This the physiology students did. At first Franz joined gleefully in their linguistic torment, but at some point his attention wandered and alit on an old monk still perched on his mercy seat, mutely surveying the scene in the vestibule. There was something striking about this monk. Franz was about to point out the striking monk to his friends when he suddenly had the strange thought that he wanted to keep that monk for himself. On their way home Franz was relieved to hear that none of the other students had noticed the striking monk. As far as they were concerned, all the monks had come out into the vestibule to mingle with their visitors, not one of them had stayed behind on his mercy seat. Franz let them believe that. At home he tried to figure out what was so striking about this one particular monk. At last he figured it out. What was so striking about the monk was that his eyes, in contrast to those of the other monks, which were either wholly vacant or else filled with love, had a skeptical, secular glint in them. The question thus became: *What was a man with such a skeptical, secular glint in his eyes doing within the walls of a monastery? Why would such a man renounce the world?* Franz kept up with his physiological studies, kept critiquing language with his friends at the coffeehouse, kept caring for his mother, who ever since a neurological incident some years earlier could only communicate her wishes to him by gesturing with the ring finger of her left hand at a large sheet of paper on which he had drawn highly simplified representations of everything in the world she could conceivably desire. More and more of his mental energy went, however, to the monk. To the monk's eyes. To the skeptical, secular glint in them. What was the man doing there? What had happened to him? Could someone with eyes like that really take seriously the vows he had taken? Everything about his eyes indicated that he stood psychically at an ironic remove from the very institution he was forbidden physically to leave . . . The glint in the monk's eyes steadily displaced everything else in Franz's life. He fell behind in his studies; he lost interest in the critique of language, which, it seemed to him in subsequent meetings, was digging up and flinging away more and more bits of language that were actually still living, leaving a linguistic skin so scanty, so inadequate, that when it was draped over reality and pulled taut it was perforated in multiple places by a reality that could no longer be contained by it; and when his mother wailed because what she wanted to express to him appeared nowhere on her sheet of paper, he, instead of frantically adding to it as he had in the past, asked her to content herself please with what was there . . . At sundown Franz would go to the monastery. Even in the near darkness of a Cistercian church at vespers one could just make out the skeptical, secular glint in the old monk's eyes. When Franz finally worked up the nerve to ask the man how he had come to be a monk, the man merely smiled, a smile that was itself strikingly skeptical and secular . . . The monks never proselytized, nor did they push Franz away, they were happy to let him sit and watch, though it must have been obvious to them that Franz was taking none of what they were saying seriously . . . Nowhere else was everyone so indifferent to his presence, especially not at home, where it had been a long time since his presence was a matter of indifference! . . . Around this time he observed that his mother's demands had begun to irritate him. There was a kind of demand he could satisfy (another glass of water) and a kind he could not (some inexpressible wish)—*both* kinds irritated him. Only the second kind pained him but both kinds irritated him. How many glasses of water could one woman drink, how many things could she want that she couldn't express? . . . He found himself avoiding home, class, the coffeehouse . . . How nice it was to sit unnoticed in the dark of the church, his mind fastened on the mystery of the monk's eyes! . . . Yet evidently he was not unnoticed, or not completely, for at some point the abbot shaved the hair off the crown of his head and stuck a soft black hat on him, the soft black hat of a Cistercian novice, and pulled a tunic onto him, too, this must have been a few years in . . . Before Franz could object the abbot had clad him also in a scapular and cincture and the brethren had encircled him to sing psalms signifying the cutting of ties to his past life and his reception into the monastic familia. By then it felt too late to say anything. Because they would say—and with good reason—why didn't you say something before the cincture, before the scapular? Before the tunic, before the hat? Before we shaved your head? And he realized, as he watched the monk in whose eyes he'd taken such a keen interest, and who, Franz noted, was not only not singing but wasn't even moving his mouth (!), and who was regarding him with a spirit of unmistakable irony (!!), that being a novice offered him an excellent vantage point from which to continue his investigation into this man's skeptical, secular glint and his reason for being here . . . In time Franz took his temporary vows, and was clothed accordingly, new cincture, new scapular, new tunic, new hat, and then he took his solemn vows, and was clothed accordingly. Never, however, did he take any of these vows seriously . . . And all the while he continually communicated to the old monk the fact that he, too, was a man of science, he, too, took this new life of his lightly, not seriously, and would therefore understand anything the old monk might wish to share about why he was here. But the latter responded to all these invitations with the same skeptical, secular smile . . . At some point Franz sent an anonymous letter to the municipal authorities in regard to his mother, and evidently they did pay a visit to the apartment, for a few days later he was able to read in all of the newspapers about what they found there . . . Some of the more scandalmongering papers even ran photographs of what was found there . . . These photos were strangely compelling . . . The interesting thing is that until he saw those photographs Franz had never thought of his mother as a physically beautiful person . . . He slipped some of these newspapers under the door of the old monk's cell, just beside his own, and after that the monk adopted a noticeably different attitude toward him . . . A noticeably friendlier attitude . . . Early one morning there was a knock on Franz's door. It was the old monk. He was holding a newspaper. Not one of the ones Franz had given him, a much older one, faded and frayed. This, said the monk, indicating a long article titled "Account of a Young Woman Wrongfully Incarcerated," is the reason I am here, if you want to know. Read it, if you want to know! Only now did Franz realize that besides the skepticism and secularism there was a third thing in the old monk's eyes that he could not yet identify. Aloud? he asked. In your head, please! cried the monk. In your head! Only, permit me to watch you as you read it.

The monk fastened his eyes on Franz's face, and Franz read the "Account of a Young Woman Wrongfully Incarcerated," of which now, many years later, he is still able to provide the following paraphrase:

I, Hilde von F—, née M—, daughter of Otto M— and Anna M—, née N—, from V—, though by disposition a private person, find myself compelled by circumstance to offer the public this brief account of my life in order to inquire whether I may have any recourse against the offenses committed against me by several individuals ostensibly responsible for safeguarding my welfare. I was born on the 22nd of September, 187–. Until the 14th of March, 188–, my childhood could be called not only happy but completely so. We lived in a large house in the liveliest district of V— and summered at an estate in Z—. My father, whose name would not be unfamiliar to readers who keep abreast of developments in physics, was a brilliant scientist, my mother a competent amateur artist. So we were given to understand. Their marriage, my brother and I were given to understand, was exemplary, enlightened, the perfect soil for the flourishing of my father's genius. Our parents doted on one another and on us. Our happy home was filled with beauty and truth. So we were given to understand. Much of this would have to be reevaluated later on.

On the 14th of March, 188–, my father, who, as my brother and I were given to understand, had, through pure mathematical intuition, discovered the hidden substructure of all real and theoretical substances, constituted by a certain particle whose behavior he captured in a simple equation, delivered at the Institute of Physics a public lecture on this subject, after which an eminent old professor of philosophy, who even now, in death, holds tremendous sway over the young, raised his hand and stated that he could no more accept our father's mathematical argument for the existence of unobservables than he could St. Anselm's argument for the existence of God. Where are these particles? said Professor von F—. If you cannot show me them, I cannot believe in them! Laughter, according to Father. After that the city turned against unobservables. What could be seen was all the rage. Wherever he went Father heard people laughing about unobservables in general and about his particles in particular. At home he repeatedly stated that he was sustained only by his family's belief in his unobservable particles. If not for my and my brother's belief in his particles, our sincere, informed belief in his unobservable particles, and the mathematics undergirding them, he would, he said, have done away with himself a long time ago, and to show that this wasn't merely a figure of speech he once led my brother and me (we were eight and nine, or nine and ten) to the second-floor window from which he would have done it. But for the grace of you two! Father said, grasping the crossbar and giving it a shake. My brother, who now, of course, claims to have no memory of this incident, was, as I recall, confused, for surely this wasn't high enough to die. I had to explain to him afterward that Father would have hanged himself from the window, not thrown himself out of it. He had shaken the crossbar to show that it would have held him. As no doubt it would have. And probably that would have been for the best.

Instead, Father proposed that we live year-round at our estate in Z— so he could study his particles in peace. Mother was reluctant. The effect on the three of us of dwelling in the woods during the darkest part of the year could scarcely be known in advance. (Three, not four, because my brother, though one year my junior, would be sent instead to an academy; hence his ignorance of the events in Z—.) What would happen in the woods, in the dark? And where, moreover, would she paint? But between my mother's hobbyistic production of still lifes and my father's inquiry into the most basic unit of nature there could, of course, be no competition; once the notion had taken hold of Father it was as good as decided that we would move to the country. Yet he had always worked hard to take my mother's interest in art seriously, as seriously as he could, and this was quite in line with his encouragement of her involvement in various municipal associations for the advancement of women. Hence he pledged, first thing, to find her a studio.

Close by the estate was an old corn mill in a state of dilapidation. Father and I went to speak to the miller. The miller was too drunk to speak but when the miller's wife heard why Father had come she asked him to repeat it three times and then fell to her knees and kissed his hands. The mill had been their ruin. The previous occupant, who had been almost as forthright with them as she would now be with us, had informed them that according to legend something terrible had once happened in it. No one knew what it was. And whatever it was it had happened long ago. But on occasion faint singing could still be heard in it. A girl's voice, and the baritone of a man. The singing was soft and beautiful but obviously demonic. Nevertheless, the previous occupant had told them, this inexplicable singing, unnerving as it is, has zero effect on the cornmeal. Everything he told us was true, the miller's wife told us, except for the last part. The miller, who I thought had fallen asleep, for he sat slumped in a chair with his eyes shut, suddenly banged the table with his fist and cried: It wasn't true that the corn was unaffected! And he pro-

ceeded to enumerate all the strange effects of the singing
on their cornmeal and corn flour. On the quality, color,
and consistency of their corn products. He had expected
their minds to be affected, but not their corn products. And
the miller could afford for his head to be affected, that was
even expected of him, when you live in a mill in the middle
of the woods everyone expects you and your wife to be a
little touched in the head, hazard of the trade, whether or
not your mill whispers now and then with ghostly, inexplicable song. And you'll happily buy your corn products
from a miller whose head is a little touched, right? But
you'd never *dream* of buying corn products from a miller
whose *corn* is a little touched! A miller who is not quite
right in the head, sure, no problem, what miller isn't, but
a miller who is not quite right in the corn? No, right? He
looked at Father. No, Father agreed. And you, dearie—
the miller squatted in front of me—you'd eat the corn of
a miller who is touched in the head but not of one who is
touched in the corn? I looked up at Father. Yes, Father
said. Even if the corn's only a little touched, right? Even
so, Father agreed. And as a matter of fact, the miller concluded, our corn was more than a *little* touched . . . The
miller's wife put a hand on her husband's shoulder, for
he was taking their rustic forthrightness slightly too far
now, to the point of risking the sale, so the miller hastened
to add: Of course, the singing works its strange effects
only on things that live, people and plants and suchlike.
It won't affect your instruments in the least. (Father had
told them he intended to use their mill as a scientific stor-
age facility, because he couldn't exactly tell them that the
means of their livelihood would be turned into a wealthy
amateur's art space. The worst thing you can do with the

means of a man's livelihood, he'd explained to me before we went in, is turn it into an art space. He added: I say this as a confirmed admirer of your mother's pretty paintings!)

When we left, Father advised me to say nothing to Mother about the nonsense with the singing. There is no question it admits of a scientific, probably meteorological, explanation, he said. The whistling of the föhn wind through the mill wheel or some such thing. But you know your mother, he said: Even if she understood the cause of it, it would make her uneasy. I vowed to say nothing. Mother moved her easel into the mill. After the first day she pronounced the mill a perfectly adequate studio. She made no mention of any singing. On the second day she said that the mill was actually ideal for her purposes and gave my father a peck on the cheek. Still no mention of any demoniacal song. On the third day Mother took all of her meals in the mill, and on the fourth day I watched from my window as she hauled her bedding into it. At supper on the fifth day Father (who, meanwhile, brooded mathematically on his unobservable particles, the existence of which I was now on an almost hourly basis asked catechetically to affirm) observed that Mother, whom we had not seen in a night and a day, evidently found the corn mill "inspiring."

At noon on the sixth day she interrupted our lesson, such as it was, to announce that on the white walls of the mill she had created an altarpiece depicting the martyrdom of St. Wolfgang, which, exactly three hours from now, we were invited to view. This development perturbed Father inasmuch as Mother was of Jewish extraction and had never shown the least interest in Catholic iconography. It was also a source of concern to him that St. Wolfgang had not been martyred but had died of natural causes on the banks of the Danube near Eferding in Upper Austria. I saw that a fearful surmise was taking form in his head—a conviction even—but he did not express it to me. He said only that he would go to see Mother's altarpiece alone. In lieu of our afternoon lesson I was to take a stroll in the mountains, to let the trees be my tutors, to climb higher and higher until I had crossed the tree line, and to wait there until I received a signal to return home. The signal would be smoke rising from the chimney of the villa. Under no circumstances was I to return before I saw the smoke. Did I understand? Yes, Father. I went up into the mountains. When I rose above the tree line I turned to face our property below, sat down in the dirt, and waited. I did not realize how much time had passed until from one moment to the next night fell. I knew that I would not be able to see smoke in the dark but I was less afraid of enduring a frigid night alone in the high mountains than of disobeying Father's orders. Three different doctors have since informed me that my survival that night is a physiological miracle. When the sun came up again I saw that smoke was rising from the chimney. I went back down.

Father was doing mathematics at the kitchen table. Had I enjoyed my nature walk? Yes, Father. Had I learned a great deal from the trees? Yes, Father. My particles? They exist, Father. Hilde, he said, your mother is whitewashing the walls of the old corn mill, which, at her suggestion, will be turned into a scientific laboratory. She has expressed a wish to help me prove the existence of my particles empirically, by means of an actual and quite ordinary substance, which I am having shipped here from the mines of J——. Empirically means: from experience. Yes, Father. And, I added, the altarpiece . . . ? It'll be best, Hilde, if you don't speak to her of the altarpiece. For the moment she has decided to be done with art. As you know, I have always admired your mother's urge to express herself, and encouraged it, for I think it a healthy and human thing, self-expression, but with this ambitious altarpiece she seems to have come up against the limitations of her talent and felt that collision painfully. I tried to point out the parts that were nicely done, but your mother is too proud to be condescended to and has decided for now to be done with art, and probably it is for the best. My particles? They exist, Father, I said, and I left as if to go to my room.

Instead I crept out of the villa and hurried to the mill. The whitewashing was almost done but one small corner of one wall remained, and in this corner, depicting the anguished reaction of an immense crowd of children to something that had already been painted over, presumably the martyrdom, I saw the truth about my mother's art: That it was good. That it was great. I suddenly understood that the fearful surmise I'd seen forming in my father's head was just this, that the old corn mill had made my mother's art great. Although whether the mill had made it great or merely permitted us to see its greatness I did not and still do not know. Either way, it was clear now that the truth value of the proposition at the heart of my life had to be flipped: My mother was the brilliant artist, my father the competent (or even incompetent) scientist. The world was inverted. Her art was good and his particles didn't exist, the math didn't even make sense. Just then Mother noticed me through the window, paled like one of the figures she had painted, and, brandishing her wet white brush, mouthed: *Go home!* I ran back to the villa. Father met me in the doorway. My particles? They exist, Father, I said as I edged past him. He laughed hollowly. Never again did he dare ask me about his particles. He must have seen that his hold over me had dissolved. The consequences of that would have to be borne by my mother.

The substance from the mines of J——, which I soon saw was far from ordinary, and blackened any surface it stood on, came the next day in a crate. Father saw to it that it was Mother who handled it; he only thought about it, she actually touched it. His protocols put her in constant close proximity to it. To watch them do their "experiments" was to watch Father sit in an easy chair while Mother was sent back and forth across the mill cradling the substance in her arms. Her flimsily gloved hands blackened by the substance. The substance depleting her. I found strands of her hair on the floor. Her own fingers, I showed her, were turning black. She denied all of this. I would not have thought it possible to deny, but she denied it. Soon Mother hardly existed apart from the substance. She declared that she felt stimulated by her scientific work with the substance. But what she was asked to do with the substance was not science. Can you not see that? Can't you see that Father has no interest in the composition of a particular substance, only of all possible substances? Can't you see that your hands are black? She could not. She raised a finger, tilted her head, and smiled: *The singing!*

It could no longer be denied that by means of this substance Father meant to murder her. When I saw that she had only a couple of days left to live, I fled to V—. I couldn't bear to watch her die. I found my brother at his academy and told him what Father had done. He with all the new authority of his formal education informed me that what I was describing was science, that that was what science looked like. I went to numerous universities, institutes, learned societies, and was told over and over again that this is what science looks like. But this was not science, murder isn't science. I went to the police and told them everything. They listened carefully and took detailed notes but only until I came to the old corn mill, at which point they glanced at one another and put down their pens. It was the same with all the municipal authorities, I invariably lost them at the corn mill, they believed me until the corn mill and doubted me after. But to tell the story without the old corn mill, without the central element of the whole causal nexus, was to sound like a lunatic in a different respect. And simply to relate the conclusion ("On an estate in Z— you will find the body of a woman with blackened fingers buried beneath an old corn mill whose whitewashed walls conceal an altarpiece depicting the unhistorical martyrdom of St. Wolfgang"), without relating all the events leading up to it, was to sound like a lunatic in still another respect. Even the sanest individual will sound mad if obliged to tell a strange-enough tale. So I stopped telling it. I stopped saying anything at all.

One day I found myself staring at a street peddler. It was the miller! Only sober now, and at peace. He'd found his calling in carving playthings for children, into whose hearts the singing had given him special insight. He had not had children of his own but on leaving the corn mill he realized that he now knew what it was every child longs for. The toys were each wooden winged figures with a hole on the head into which a candle could be put. Here, dearie! And he gave me three of them. I told him what my father had done to my mother. His smile disappeared. Did he believe me? Of course. Yes. He gave me a fourth figure and a fifth, explained where to put the candles (in the heads), and pushed his cart up the street.

Fortified by this encounter, I renounced my silence. I wrote to the great philosopher Professor von F——. His reply did *not* say that what I had seen was science. With characteristic integrity he was not prepared without more evidence to say that it was murder, but he was certain it wasn't science. An exchange ensued, culminating in a most unexpected but not unwelcome way, with a wedding announcement in this very periodical. The space being ours to do with as we wished, we included in the announcement a few lines in remembrance of my mother and an emphatic denial of the existence of my father's particles. The next morning, three doctors and three policemen forced their way into my quarters, followed by my father playing to perfection the role of a broken man brought to grief by an impossible daughter. As I was led through the rain to a waiting carriage he wept and wailed that he had failed me and that this would be in my own best interest. Nothing, not even the colossal diamond ring Professor von F—— had already picked out for me from the court jeweler, could induce my minders to turn the carriage around.

At the Sanatorium Dr. Krakauer, the institution to which I was taken, the man for whom the place is named scarcely looked me up and down before declaring me morally insane. I had not said a word to him. It is certain he was paid handsomely in advance. On his orders I am given medication eight times a day, which, besides all that it does to my mind, causes excruciating pain in my abdomen. I tell his assistant physicians my story over and over again, but it is clear to me now that my father engineered everything so ingeniously that the straightforward recitation of the facts is sufficient to cast my sanity in doubt. Only by this means could he neutralize the one witness to my mother's murder. If, as he maintains, she is still alive, then, I tell him, show her to me! It is very simple: Let me see her. But this, of course, is the one thing he cannot do. He can write me letters in her hand, he can parade actresses before me, but he cannot show me my mother. My brother, meanwhile, remains in his sway. My husband is dead. I am alone. So I am compelled to address myself to the public. Is it really possible, I want to know, for a doctor to diagnose a person as morally insane before she has said a single word? Is he authorized by the law to incarcerate her on such grounds? And does there exist some substance, some solvent, that can dissolve a layer of whitewash while leaving intact any images underneath?

Anyone with answers to these questions was kindly requested to write to the author care of the Sanatorium Dr. Krakauer, the address of which, Father Franz recalls, concluded the article.

Franz looked up. The old monk was smiling. Crazy, no? And what he found craziest, Father Franz recalls him saying, wasn't even the claim itself, for by then he was already well versed in his daughter's inventions, but the fact that a newspaper agreed to print it. And even more than this, that some people took it seriously. He sued the paper for slander, and won. A retraction was published that disclosed Hilde M——'s tragic history of mendacity, shamelessness, adventure seeking, and perversion. A note from Dr. Krakauer offered some neurological insight into her condition and a letter to the editor from Hilde's brother attested to the fact, mad to have to state, that their mother was still very much alive.

Yet even all this, Father Franz recalls the old monk saying, would not, for certain people, be sufficient. He knew that. For certain people, all of this was the wrong kind of evidence. His marshaling of these legal, medical, and familial forces would only validate the suspicions about him implanted in them by his daughter, the tale she had spun. He knew that. People like that would never be satisfied unless they could see for themselves that there were no images beneath the whitewash, no bones beneath the floor. Even when the world moved on from all this, as it soon did, there would always be a certain kind of person of a certain sort of temperament—a temperament with which he, as a scientist, was actually in sympathy—who would still wonder whether there was something beneath the whitewash, something underneath the floor. Images, bones. He was advised by everyone with an interest in his welfare not to concern himself any longer with the kind of person who could not be convinced. For even if he invited the public to the mill, as he was now talking about doing, and stripped the whitewash right in front of them, and pried up the floorboards, and let the public see for itself that there were no images, no bones, the kind of person with whom he was preoccupied would not be convinced. For someone committed to believing them his daughter's accusations could never be conclusively disproven, he knew that, since bones could always be moved, or ground down to dust, and images destroyed. There would never be an end to it. It is exhausting, he thought, to have a child. He decided to let the matter drop.

Years passed. His daughter died. Eventually he decided that something, however small, would in fact be gained by compelling everyone to admit at least that there were no bones *here*, no images *here*. At three o'clock on a certain summer day anyone interested was invited to join him in the corn mill, where, using a solvent of his own invention, he would strip the whitewash from the walls, and then pry up the floorboards to show that there were no bones underneath. By that time no one remembered the business with the daughter and so no one knew what he was talking about. But probably for that reason the mill was packed. If he had said that there *were* bones beneath the mill probably no one would have showed up, but because he said there'd be *no* bones, everyone showed up. Probably they thought there would be bones. And images. It was almost a pity to disappoint them.

But something strange happened: when he stripped off the whitewash, there were images underneath it, and when he pulled up the floorboards, there were bones. This was the only moment of his life that could properly be called mystical. He went straight to the police but they could not understand for what crime he wished to be arrested, and when they did understand would not do it. From the police station he came to the monastery. Later of course he was able to rationalize what he had seen: the bones were small, not those of a grown woman; the images, too, were like the scratchings of a child; and both seemed ancient, perhaps a hundred years old. Certainly they had nothing to do with him.

Even the mystical feeling that gripped him and impelled him here when the law wouldn't take him was completely explicable in psychological terms. There was nothing that still needed explaining, and nothing here that would have helped him explain anything anyway. But by the time he came to that realization he had come to like it at the monastery. It's pleasant here, no? Aha! cried the old monk, for the bells had now, in Father Franz's recollection, begun to ring. Matins!

The third thing in the old monk's eyes, besides the skepticism and the secularism, was a degree of self-absorption Franz had encountered nowhere else on earth and which instilled in him a horror that persists to this day.

For he knew then and still knows today that at any moment he could succumb to self-absorption to precisely the same degree.

Everything Father Franz has done since has been done with the aim of avoiding that fate: Quitting the monastery. Joining the priesthood. Ministering to his flock. A constant turning away from the self and toward the world. Opening himself up more and more to the world. Other people, other things. Letting more and more of it in. And finally letting all of it in, ingesting all of it, opening himself up all the way and ingesting the whole world, in the form of its waste material. The dissolution of the self through the absorption of the (waste of the) world. It was a good thing, a *good* thing, that was going to happen at the end of the day, physically painful (for how would it fit in him?) but good and proper, fair recompense for his sins, and precisely the opposite—though he hardly expected Dr. Krakauer to understand this!—of narcissism.

He left.

A moment later he reappeared. If, he said, you write down the tale I've just told you and send it to the city, I think your little Gretel might enjoy it. What! Don't look so surprised! What else do you think you talk about all day! The walls are paper thin, and you mutter while you write! Oh, don't be embarrassed, it is a pleasure to hear the prayers of a father so devoted to his daughter! Yes, that's what they are, prayers! Until now you've shielded her from the evils of the world, and now it is up to God! But the truth is, it was always up to God, even when it was just you and Gretel! Good morning! he cried, and he went to lie down on his bed, from which (and it is dark as I write this) he hasn't risen again since.

Narcissism, catatonia, and moral insanity, indeed! Father Franz is quite mad. Yet his tale, provided you take none of it seriously, might amuse you, I thought. So here it is.

Good night!

G

THE GENERAL INTENDANT'S DAUGHTER GRACES THE STAGE IN *THE GLASSWORKER* . . .

The girl's expressive gifts surpass those of all the members of his company, even the aging starlet Klamt. That is something the General Intendant of the City Theater can no longer deny.

To this point he has done everything in his power to keep his daughter off the stage, for the General Intendant is intimately acquainted with the unscrupulousness of theater people and is well aware that if he casts her in a leading role she will be subjected to the most malicious slander.

And so will he.

But in light of her expressive gifts, which have now achieved a perfection he once hardly thought possible, he must concede that withholding them from the city whose theatrical life he has sworn to cultivate (but which under his supervision has grown only more decadent) would be an intolerable abdication of his duty.

The General Intendant therefore risks the opprobrium of the public, and the rage of Klamt the aging starlet, by commissioning a play for his daughter to star in, one especially suited to her expressive gifts, the action of which should include, he suggests to the dramatist, the following basic elements:

The curtain should rise on a man in a straitjacket scrutinizing the large stained glass window in the altar of the chapel of a psychiatric facility. The man, who for some time has existed in a perpetual present tense, suddenly remembers that *he himself*, in his prior life as a glassworker, created this stained glass window, which depicts five female saints decapitated for their faith. He marvels at the fact that he, who now feels so far from the beautiful, was once capable of bringing such beauty into the world. As he studies the window, the man feels an urge he has not felt in a very long time: the urge to bring more beauty into the world. If the man cannot bring more beauty into the world, through his mastery of the craft of glasswork, he would rather die. The man proclaims as much to a chapel that the audience has thus far taken for empty. But from the two wings two stout old nurses appear, sharply tighten the straps of his straitjacket, which had already seemed as tight as possible, and inform the man that in this institution there is of course no opportunity to work with glass. As if they would let the inmates work with glass! The laughter of the nurses echoes in the chapel long after they have clacked away. But a glassworker who can never again work with glass is better off dead. He tries to kill himself. Of course the clinic has seen to it that he has no means of doing so. He despairs. Yet at the height of his despair more memories return to him. It was while he was installing this stained glass window that he suffered his first fit of insanity—he remembers that now. From the time of that initial fit he foresaw the fate that has since overtaken him; namely, that upon completion of the window he would be committed to this very institution for the rest of his life. He recalls realizing that while his insanity was still only intermittent he could outwit fate by means of his craft. The man had then done something to the stained glass window, or committed to memory some secret about it. *He had secretly installed it in such a way that the stained*

58

glass window would later enable him to escape by way of it. The clarity and force of this recollection thrust the man back into the third pew. But when he tries to remember what the secret of the stained glass window *is*, he cannot. Yet even this he must have foreseen, for in those first transient fits of insanity his mind was stripped of its memories and left only with such things as are common to the species. He must have known that it would not be enough to supply himself with a means of escape: he had to find a way to remind himself of the form it took and the secret of its use. He must have known that he could not entrust his memory with something as important as this. Nor could he write it down, since a written message would be confiscated on admittance. He must have relied on another person. But in the whole world, as far as the man was concerned, there was only one other person. The man suddenly recalls the existence of his beloved. He remembers teaching his beloved the words she was to say to him after he went insane and was committed here: *Your name is Gustav. You are a glassworker. The beautiful window you see before you is your own handiwork. You must simply . . . and come back to me.* Simply what? The words between *simply* and *come back to me*, the very words the man needs most, have been expunged from his mind. He recalls drilling his beloved again and again until she could recite the words without error. Yet his beloved has never been to visit him. Where is his beloved? What has happened to her? He confides in the chief physician about his beloved. Not about the message she was to deliver, only about her existence. But even this is a mistake, for the chief physician (to be played by the great actor and tenor Silberberg) lets it be known that he wants to hear nothing more about the beloved, in whose existence he plainly disbelieves. No one at the facility believes in the existence of the beloved—no one, that is, except the two stout old nurses, who up until now have struck us as cruel and unfeeling crones, and one of whom is to be played by the aging starlet Klamt. In the middle of the night the nurses enter the man's room and convey their belief in the existence of the beloved. They pledge to locate the beloved. Lo and behold, they do locate her. They bring the beloved to him. But can this be she? *This* is his beloved?! The man weeps. His beloved exists now in a lamentable state. She cannot walk. She cannot speak. Only her eyes move to and fro. Yet the movement of her eyes, even from the very last row of the balcony of the City Theater, is extraordinarily expressive. To the attentive theatergoer this movement of the beloved's eyes expresses everything that needs to be known about her relationship to the man. The one thing it cannot express, however, is the secret message she was supposed to impart to him. This secret message is locked within his quasi-vegetative beloved. He therefore sets out to do what not only the chief physician but even the nurses try to tell him is impossible: to teach his beloved to speak again. He brings her to the chapel. Positions her cane-backed wheelchair before the altar. *My name*, he tells her, *is Gustav. I am a glassworker. The beautiful window you see before you is my own handiwork. I must simply . . . and come back to you.* Hour after hour with remarkable tenderness and devotion he says these words to his beloved, always pausing long enough at the ellipsis for her to leap in and impart with miraculously restored speech the secret of the stained glass window. But she never leaps in. Her speech is never restored. Only her eyes move to and fro, to and fro, in a manner that is exquisitely expressive, but not of the right thing. Now visiting hours are over. The clacking of the nurses gets louder and louder. They are coming to the chapel to take away his beloved. He knows that they will not bring her back. Not ever. He tries one last time: *My name is Gustav. I am a glassworker. The beautiful window you see before you is my own handiwork. I must simply . . .* He pauses. She says nothing. Yet this time—and it does seem to him a miracle even if it is not the one he expected—he is able to whisper the missing words himself. *I must simply smash my head hard through the glass and come back to you.* Now the man shatters the glass by thrusting the crown of his head through the middlemost of the five female saints. As blood streams down his face he kisses his beloved on the lips and then climbs through the opening where the window had been. He is now free to bring more beauty into the world. The nurses enter the chapel. Their clacking ceases. For a moment the theater is absolutely silent. Then the beloved, her face streaked with blood, suddenly leaps to her feet and screams: *Your name is Bohuslav! You are a bricklayer!* The implication is that he—who is to be played by the City Theater's most physically massive actor—is responsible for her condition and is now free to commit more crimes. But this is something the attentive theatergoer will have long since deduced from the movement to and fro of her eyes. The nurses, who do not remark on the shattered window and actually seem hardly to notice it, now wheel the beloved out of the chapel. As they do so, the General Intendant suggests, the curtain should fall. Of course, he leaves the particulars to the imagination of the dramatist.

The malicious slander anticipated by the General Intendant begins as soon as the cast list of *The Glassworker* is pinned to the wall and Klamt discovers that instead of the Beloved she is to play one of the two stout sixty-five-year-old nurses. And that the Beloved is to be played by the daughter of the General Intendant.

The gist of the slander, which can no doubt be traced back to Klamt, is that the infirmities and limitations of the character of the Beloved are also those of the General Intendant's daughter. That the daughter cannot walk, that she cannot speak, that she expresses herself with her eyes only because she is unable to express herself by any other means. That *The Glassworker* has been contrived specifically so as to allow her father to cast her in it. That only a play in which the leading lady is absent from Act I and sits mute and motionless for nearly all of Act II is one that could even conceivably feature the General Intendant's daughter at the top of the bill.

This malicious slander pains the General Intendant. But it moves him to see how little it seems to pain his daughter. She could of course disprove it in an instant. She would only have to stand up or speak. One word would be sufficient. What gives this slander some purchase is her determination to do no such thing. To rehearse the role of the Beloved completely in character. To have her father wheel her into the City Theater every morning and wheel her out again at night. To have him lift her onto the stage in his arms. To communicate with no one, not even with him, not even one word. There is even a part of him that envies the degree to which her commitment to her art leaves her indifferent to the world and its scorn.

The world is something to which he himself, both as a father and as an arts administrator, has not for a long time been in a position to be indifferent.

And he is not indifferent to this. The General Intendant gathers his company. It is true that *The Glassworker* is contrived, he says: It is contrived to remind you how much an actor can express with even the smallest gesture. The simplest gesture. *The Glassworker* is indeed contrived: Contrived to remind the people of the city of the power of the Theater, to remind us in the Theater of the power of our art. A power we have all forgotten.

The company murmurs.

But given the daughter's refusal to disprove the slander, it does not go away. It only intensifies. It is whispered, presumably first by Klamt, that anything expressed in her eyes is in fact without meaning or intent and bears only an accidental relation to the text of *The Glassworker*. That her baffled expression isn't acting, it is actual bafflement. That her horrified expression is actual horror. That when the General Intendant (who receives special permission from the director to join each rehearsal as a kind of informal codirector) devotes all of his codirecting energy to directing his daughter, and in particular to directing, or codirecting, her eyes—which must convey to even the last row of the balcony that that man is no glassworker, he's a bricklayer, and what he's brought into the world is a far cry from beauty—that those hours and hours of rehearsal time are gone, simply gone.

How, the General Intendant points out to his company, if you honestly believe the cruel things that you say, do you suppose she will be able to leap to her feet at the climax of the play and exclaim, *Your name is Bohuslav! You are a bricklayer!*

The company murmurs. That's true. But it is pointed out by Klamt in turn that the scene in which the Beloved exclaims *Your name is Bohuslav! You are a bricklayer!* is the one scene that is never rehearsed.

Finally, and in front of the whole company, the General Intendant kneels before his daughter in her chair and begs her with tears in his eyes and his head in her lap to break character. Not for her sake, he knows she doesn't care what they think, but for his!

He is weak! He does care! But when she doesn't break character even to decline what he begs of her, he tells the company that he is proud of his daughter and ashamed of himself. Only someone so committed to her role and so indifferent to the world is entitled to call herself an actor.

After this the malicious slander about her expressive gifts is repeated less often, and less gleefully.

Not, however, by Klamt, who if anything only escalates her abuse.

Klamt claims that the General Intendant does not even come from the world of drama. He comes from the world of dance. He impaired his wife with dance! Slew her with an undanceable dance! A dance no one could dance! So first of all they were taking their dramaturgical guidance from someone who had zero formal training in theater! And who murdered his wife through choreography! This in the opinion of the finest physicians! But of course she wasn't, *by his lights*, dead. No, he took her home. Sustained her somehow, though not in a way anyone would wish to be sustained. Saw an opportunity in all this: A dance opportunity! An opportunity to "start from scratch" dancewise! Didn't have the decency to let her die, had to make her keep dancing instead! Of course this dance didn't pan out. At first there was promise. Her movements struck him as entirely new. Or rather— old! Primordial! From a stage in the development of the human organism that preceded our fall into sociality and culture and the stink of the city! Never mind whether they could really be called "dance movements"! He was struck above all by one movement. At intervals a finger shot to her now bald brow and traced an arc across the side of her skull. A prehistoric gesture, he thought! The meaning of which was inscrutable to him! Must stem from the innate nature of man! Upon this one primeval movement an entire school of dance could be founded! But no. One day he notices a painting painted of them on the eve of their wedding in which she is making the very same movement. Coquettishly tucking a strand of hair behind one ear. Now there was no hair on her head and possibly no essence to her person but the fashionable world is still moving her muscles! There is no "preceding our fall into sociality"! No escape from "the stink of the city"! No "prehistory"! No "starting from scratch"! Not once you've walked even one city block! He decides to have another child by her. Doesn't know whether this is possible. Finds that it is! This one he raises properly! Pristinely! In the dark! In the midst of the city but sheltered from the gestural tyranny of the city! Food through a slot, water through a hole and into a shallow trough! Sheltered from a city which without our knowing it is always telling us how to move and how not to! Enters only when she is sleeping so as not to influence her with his movements! Wants nothing more than to embrace her tiny sleeping form but restrains himself in case upon waking she retains a memory of that motion! By a thousand such self-sacrifices ensures that hers is the first childhood free from violence! No movement possibilities are foreclosed to her! Everything is possible! She can move any which way! How his daughter chooses to move is for the first time in the history of man a genuine choice! Now he simply waits to see how she will choose to move! How she will choose to dance! But—she chooses *not* to move! She chooses *not* to dance! She chooses to sit! Or else (Klamt has heard it told both ways!) the way in which she chooses to move and dance obliges him to inhibit her movements by means of straps, for her own sake, after which, even once free again, she ceases to move! Whatever the case: After a certain point, there is no movement! No dancing! Yet he cannot quite disabuse himself of the notion that she is, for all that, a dancer! To admit that his daughter is no dancer is to admit that the way he raised her may not have been in her best interest! Only in time does he disabuse himself of the notion that she is a dancer! And only by means of another notion onto which he's able to transfer the same psychological load: that she is an actor . . .

Now Klamt has gone too far. The members of the company turn away from her in disgust. Imagine reacting so poorly to losing a role! And the stout old nurse is still a speaking part, that's more than most of them got!

Klamt herself becomes the subject of slander. In her increasingly baroque and frankly hysterical rumormongering, some in the company claim to detect not only the rancor of an ousted starlet but the rage of a jilted lover, an innuendo the General Intendant asks them to rise above but also does not explicitly dispel.

Meanwhile a consensus begins to form among the members of the company that the daughter's performance is "powerful."

Rumors of her expressive gifts spread beyond the walls of the City Theater. Before the public has even seen her onstage she becomes the recipient of an outpouring of adoration.

And on the night of the premiere she leaps to her feet at the climax of the play and exclaims, *Your name is Bohuslav! You are a brick-layer!* The company is willing to testify to that, the audience is willing to testify to that. She leapt to her feet and exclaimed, *Your name is Bohuslav! You are a bricklayer!*—the whole city is willing to testify to that, no one will deny it.

No one, that is, apart from the aging starlet Klamt. Again and again she refuses—and loudly!—to admit it. Eventually she is sent to Dr. Krakauer's sanatorium. Here Klamt is asked continually by Dr. Krakauer whether it is *possible* that the General Intendant's daughter said what everyone heard her say, and Klamt just missed it. She knows that admitting this possibility would be enough to get her discharged. She simply has to say the words *It is possible that the General Intendant's daughter said the words Your name is Bohuslav, you are a bricklayer* and that night she would sleep in her own bed. And privately she will admit that of course it is possible, anything is possible. But Klamt, too, is committed to her role.

H

THE HOTELIER HAS TO PLAY THE HAPPY HOSTESS TO HURT
THE MAN WHO HURT HER HUSBAND . . .

Gretel, do you recall our cozy Christmastimes? Our fragrant tree, the toys from Egerer's? But above all the little pinewood box stamped with the seal of the Hotel H——! This, I'd remind you, was your mother's favorite confection. She had it first on our very first date. Then I'd enumerate its seven layers: The two each of marzipan and crême pâtissière, the sponge cake, the red currant preserve, and the coating of chocolate ganache. Finally it was my pleasure to watch you devour it, just as I'd watched your mother do . . .

Yes, our very first date! Oh, Gretel, how nervous I was! How eager to entertain! I took her to the Hotel H—— after a terrible show at the City Theater, which at that time was considering for production one of my earliest scripts. As we waited for the confection to arrive, I explained why, from a technical perspective, the play we had seen was without aesthetic merit, which I thought would interest your mother all the more inasmuch as she had enjoyed it. Then I enumerated the seven layers of the confection. Yet something behind me held her attention more than anything I had to say. I twisted around in my chair. An expensively bejeweled little old lady was flitting about the café, dispensing salutations and emitting peals of laughter, shadowed all the while by a large, impassive middle-aged man.

You know who that is, don't you?

Now your mother was interested!

That, I told her, is Frau H., the notorious hotelier, and her son, who still clings to the hope that his mother will one day hand the hotel over to him. You can plainly see what that hope has done to him. Listen:

Even thirty-three years after the fact, Frau H., a butcher's daughter who rose to become the proprietor of the Hotel H—, yet whose resentment of the rich is said to be undiminished and without peer, still stands accused in the eyes of the city of driving her husband to his grave. They say that even though she married him for his wealth she could never forgive the ease with which he came into it. One afternoon his father signed the hotel over to him and she, it is said, lost her mind. He gaily waved the paper with his father's signature and she was never again the same in the head. She thought of her own father with his meat cleaver and his poverty and felt that it fell to her to impose a cost on her husband for what he'd obtained for free. What's worse, he had no business running this high-end hotel, because his rich clientele held no interest for him. He was interested instead—albeit only on a theoretical level—in the plight of the poor, about whom he read a great many books. He was always comparing what he read in these books to the experience of her childhood, always asking her whether it was true that the poor did this or that, lived like this or that, held this or that belief, to which she, in order to bring such conversations to as swift a conclusion as possible, always replied: Yes. Whereas she, precisely because she so resented the rich, was fascinated by them, understood them, and, according to the city's prevailing psychological wisdom, loved them. She was the ideal person to run such a high-end hotel. Only someone with such hatred of the rich would wish to spend a lifetime catering to their whims, according to the neat perversities of the prevailing psychology. She decided not merely to impose a cost on her husband for his hotel but to dispossess him of the hotel and dispose of him altogether. It is said that she did so by henpecking him till he killed himself. She discovered flaw after flaw in his luxury hotel, evidence of decline from the days when his father ran it. The staff was less solicitous, the cut flowers less fresh, the floors less spotless, the mattresses harder, the sheets less fine. Everywhere he looked he was made to see signs that he had failed to uphold the family hotel's standard of excellence. This was the sentiment he is said to have expressed in a brief note on hotel stationery in a sixth-floor suite before slashing his throat in the clawfoot tub. As soon as the mess was cleaned up, which, owing to the characteristically punctilious way he did the deed, took no time at all, she informed their adolescent son that while the hotel was his by rights, he would continue his apprenticeship, then in the hotel kitchen, until he could be entrusted with the entire establishment. Thirty-three years later, as is evident to anyone who sees the middle-aged man scurrying behind his high-handed mother, the apprenticeship is still ongoing. Having appropriated the hotel from the male line of its founder, she has no intention of giving it back. In these thirty-three years the standard of the hotel has been raised to a hitherto unthinkable level of excellence, but that fact induces as much guilt as pleasure in its patrons, for they know that the woman responsible for their pleasure is a murderer who has never once taken a moment to mourn her victim and continues even now to victimize his son.

So it is said, I told your mother.

The city simply doesn't know what to do with such an ambitious, impious, quintessentially modern woman, who drinks and smokes and pays so little mind to the memory of her husband, and so much to the excellence of her hotel . . .

So it is said. A rumor Frau H. herself has had reason, as you will see, not to refute. The truth, of course, I told your mother, could not be more different:

For thirty-three years, this hotelier, a humble woman of un-equaled piety, for whom the rich and the poor are equally at the mercy of God's inscrutable will, and for whom the hospitality industry means less than nothing, has mourned her beloved husband without a moment's pause. The sixth-floor suite in which he took his own life was long ago hung with black silk and turned into her private chapel to his memory, where she spends hours each morning in silent prayer. And the hotel as a whole became her instrument of retribution against the man actually respon-sible for his death. Namely, the Duke. If she drilled the staff to be ever more solicitous, if she sought out ever finer sheets, if she played the part of the spirited hostess by drinking alcohol and smoking tobacco, it was only to keep the sybaritic Duke comfort-able and content, in order to keep him close at hand. If she never spoke up to deny the horrid things the city said about her, it was only so as not to alert him to her designs. And if not for these designs she would gladly have handed the hotel over to her son a long time ago . . .

The truth is that the Duke, who as a young man was not only a sybarite but also an egoist, a nihilist, and a wastrel, fond of amusing his aristocratic friends by means of cruel jokes at the expense of their inferiors, had occasioned the death of the hote-lier's husband soon after the latter took over the hotel, when the city was still abuzz with speculation over whether he'd be able to uphold his father's standard of excellence. The Duke loudly announced in the café that the confection he'd ordered—which he'd loved since he was a boy and whose delights you, too, I told your mother, are about to discover—was "a little too rich," a patent absurdity since the confection was famous precisely for its richness. He sent it back. Everyone's eyes followed that almost untouched confection as it traveled from the Duke's table back to the kitchen. Her husband never recovered. Everywhere he looked he now perceived signs of decline. It was little use pointing out, as she frantically did, that the staff was as solicitous as ever, the cut flowers as fresh, the floors as clean, the mattresses as soft, the sheets as fine! At first this provided some solace. But soon he began muttering darkly that all of that was beside the point. He became preoccupied with an old family credo which held that the excellence of their establishment consisted not in this or that attribute or amenity but in a certain intangible quality that suffused the whole hotel. The credo had always struck him as wishful thinking or clever marketing. But now he saw the truth in it. One could not say in words what this truth was. But it was not a happy truth. For if the excellence is intangible, then there are no criteria of excellence. The floors could be scrubbed to a shine, but that had nothing to do with excellence. The staff could be made to bow and scrape, but that had nothing to do with excellence. He went from room to room feeling between thumb and forefinger the fineness of the sheets without any conviction that what he was feeling had anything to do with excellence. Perfectionism! declared the distinguished Dr. Krakauer, a frequent guest of the hotel. Without it this place would not be what it is! But such behavior, Frau H. knew, had nothing to do with the pursuit of perfection. It was just a derangement resulting from a cruel little jest intended to amuse a table of aristocrats. While inspecting a sixth-floor suite her husband reached the conclusion, recorded neatly on hotel stationery, that *nothing has anything to do with excellence*, and then took his life in the aforementioned manner, the only point where the rumor intersected the truth.

Now, if the Duke apologized for his jest, she, in her piety, was prepared to forgive him. "Who could have foreseen the consequences? None of us can presume to know the ways of the Lord!" . . . It gave her some consolation to formulate the words with which a butcher's daughter would absolve a duke before his lackeys in the middle of a frivolous, iniquitous city of which her own hotel was the apotheosis . . . But when he not only did not apologize but did not even acknowledge that it had been a jest, when, with a straight face, he repeated his claim—to grins that did not escape her even though his aristocratic friends tried their best to suppress them—that the confection had been "a little too rich," though the one he was enjoying now was evidently just fine, and then demanded sotto voce that a room be prepared for him and an actress from the City Theater, she resolved instead to serve as the means of God's vengeance against him.

She would take from the Duke something of as much value to him as her husband had been to her.

But it did not take her long to realize that he valued nothing so much. As an egoist he cared about no one but himself, and as a nihilist not even that.

She would have to wait until God had given him something of value, which she could then take away.

In the meantime she had to keep him in her clutches. So while she wanted nothing more than to grieve her husband and contemplate their reunion in the hereafter, she was compelled by circumstance to hide her widow's weeds beneath a fashionable dress and set about upholding the hotel's standard of excellence. To put on a stylish hat and fancy jewelry. To stick, for the sake of eccentricity, a cigar in her mouth. To glad-hand the rich and turn away the poor. To give every appearance of caring about a hotel. A hotel! While her son, a natural-born hotelier who cared about nothing else, who by the age of eighteen knew as much as anyone in Europe about the art of hotel management, had to be told that the apprenticeship he had begun under his father would need to continue a little while longer. So as not to make him an accessory to her crime, she could give no reason aside from saying that he still had a lot to learn about running a high-end hotel.

Thus she became a hotelier, and brought the Hotel H— to its present perfection, and the Duke never found reason to defect to another establishment.

For his romantic assignations a room was set aside for him on the sixth floor, a suite, its windows hung with black silk for absolute privacy, and with a clawfoot bathtub big enough for two.

She waited for him to fall in love with one of the actresses or ballerinas he brought up there, but that did not happen. Every night, after midnight, the Duke leaned naked out the doorway and ordered the butler to send up the house confection. For two? For one. Very good, sir. The woman and the confection would pass each other in the corridor.

As years went by the hotelier's hatred for the Duke did not lessen but she began to despair that he would ever come to care about anything in the world. Even when he married a woman of his own class the hotelier was quick to realize—after watching the two of them dine together at this very table, I told your mother—that that development had brought him no closer to having anything in his life of value to him.

One night, after the confection had gone in, and the latest paramour out, the hotelier was tempted to bring matters to a less than satisfactory conclusion by simply killing him and herself, if only to free her son from his servitude and hasten her reconciliation with her husband, but as she approached his suite holding a cleaver behind her back the door swung open and the Duke, fully dressed, declared: My wife is about to give birth!

Soon after the first there was a second, and then a third, and in the end there were seven of them, all daughters. It was said that all seven of them were daddy's girls, and that the Duke, to the considerable surprise of the entire city, worshipped and delighted in them. Indeed, they were often seen following him single file on their way to the City Theater or Natural History Museum. Still, the hotelier had reason to doubt the Duke's transformation. After all, Devoted Father was one part this dandy had not yet played, and it was clearly a hit with the public. But one afternoon, after completing her prayers, she happened to part the black silk curtains just in time to see the Duke escorting his daughters home from a matinée of the ballet. After crossing a busy street he spun round to count them: One, two, three, four, five, six. Six! Where's the seventh?! Ah, there she is, the littlest one, still on the far corner, gazing raptly at a rather garish flower arrangement. When he ran over and picked her up his relief was palpable even six floors up. As a mother, the hotelier knew very well that this could be no act, and she found herself immensely moved.

These seven daughters, then, were what she would take from him.

The next night the Duke had a rendezvous with the principal dancer. The hotelier had the kitchen whip up seven confections, and with white icing she herself adorned each with the name of a princess. Then she injected each with poison. The next morning she knocked on his door—which to her surprise was opened by the dancer—and thrust into the Duke's arms a teetering stack of wooden boxes. A treat for the girls! Don't let them have it right before bed, it's a little rich, they'll be up all night!

What the hotelier did not realize is that while the Duke's assignations with the principal dancer were not only sanctioned by his wife but even scheduled in consultation with her, he was forbidden to bring anything sweet into the house, anything that might tempt her. So as he passed by the poorhouse located halfway between the Hotel H— and the ducal residence, he was struck by a philanthropic impulse. When, the next day, the hotelier read in the papers that seven orphan boys had perished of an unknown ailment, and saw the Duke through the glass leading his brood toward the park, she had occasion to marvel at the inscrutability of Providence, and knew in her heart that justice had been done, if only on a plane to which neither she nor anyone else in this profane city had access.

She now summoned her son and told him the hotel was his, just as soon as she could announce to the public what she now disclosed to him: that his father had been slain by a member of the aristocracy by means of a quip about a confection the latter was served, which he claimed was a little too rich; that for reasons we cannot know God had marked the aristocrat and his seed for survival and accepted in their place the sacrifice of seven little orphan boys; that her son would now take over day-to-day operations of the Hotel H——, whose standard of excellence she had every confidence he would uphold; and that she herself would accept without question whatever punishment the authorities saw fit to hand down.

Her horrified son, who knew precisely what that punishment would be—that his mother would be sent to a madhouse—tried every means of dissuading her from making such an announcement, but to each of his arguments, so preoccupied with the things of this world, she replied by asking him to remember the family credo, which in her decades of prayer had never failed to bring her peace because it meant that this world is suffused by another. Only when he had exhausted his arguments did the son announce that he, too, had a confession to make: It was he, all those years ago, who had made the Duke's confection. He thought he could improve on the recipe—"For Father's sake!"—by halving the amount of sponge cake and adding a third layer of crème pâtissière. It's possible that it was in fact a little too rich; he later came to realize that three layers of crème pâtissière is one layer too many. She mustn't say a word about the orphan boys! Yes, he saw now that there's a reason the recipe is the way it is, the sponge cake serves a purpose. For a moment his mother didn't say anything. Perhaps she was wondering whether he was lying to her, for her sake. Or perhaps she was thinking about the seven little pine coffins lowered that morning into a common grave. But in the end all she said was: You still have a lot to learn about running a high-end hotel.

Just then the waiter brought my coffee and your mother's confection.

Your mother beckoned him closer. Is that, she whispered doubt-fully, pointing at the middle-aged man, really the owner's son?

Yes, the waiter replied, that's Hermann! He's a very sweet man. Mute, sadly, and a little slow, but he loves this hotel more than anyone, and Frau H. has always done all she can to make him feel involved in it. She's an angel . . .

The waiter ran off; I winked at your mother; she gave me a queer but amused look, sliced her fork into that famous confection, and offered me the first bite. I had to confess that I am one of those strange people for whom the confection holds no appeal, none, that for whatever reason (and it's not just the guilt I would feel afterward) I find it practically inedible. But I can enjoy it vicariously—I can enjoy your enjoyment! So please, I said. Go ahead. Eat.

THE IMMUNOLOGIST INTENDS TO INJECT INNUMERABLE INDIVIDUALS WITH A SERUM OF HIS OWN INVENTION . . .

A disease ravages the poor parts of the city. It travels from person to person with pitiless rapidity and has already claimed thousands of children. The rich get sick as well, but it's the poor who tend to die from it. Probably there is not a single researcher at the Pathological-Anatomical Institute who in his heart of hearts is unaware of what is happening. Everyone even knows what the disease is. But because the municipal authorities—who wring their hands over the plight of the poor but actually do the bidding of a coalition of industrialists—wish to conceal its existence, no one at the Institute, which receives its funding from the city, breathes a word about it.

And neither does the immunologist.

He keeps his mouth shut, because he has a family to feed.

Yet he is disgusted by his own silence. That for the sake of these two children he would sacrifice those of the masses. Merely because these two happen to be his own. He loves these two, and not the others, but that is a quirk of fate, it has nothing to do with right and wrong. He tries to explain this to his children but they are too young to understand what he means. Even with the help of drawings and allegorical tales of kings and princesses they cannot be brought to understand. So that they might at least know how fortunate they are he describes to them what it is like to die of the disease. How the pupils of the eyes slip upward into the head. But before he can finish the description the children are shepherded by their mother toward the bath. Only by drinking a strong clear plum brandy can he drive the fact of the disease out of his head. At some point the immunologist realizes that his children will not be returning for the bedtime kiss that had been mutually agreed upon, and for this he feels justified in raging inwardly at their mother. When at last he crawls into bed he has forgotten all about the disease and has forgiven his wife and is ready, therefore, to make love to her. She, however, has been asleep for hours. When he wakes up in the morning the fact of the disease returns to him, and he puts on his shirt and trousers and goes into the Institute, where no one, not even he, will so much as utter its name . . .

Every afternoon at a coffeehouse near the Institute, across the street from an old monastery, the immunologist reads the newspapers. One afternoon he reads about seven orphan boys claimed by the disease. Although of course the disease itself cannot be mentioned. The municipal censor sees to it that a euphemism is used. The bodies of the boys are thrown in a pauper's pit before their autopsies can be conducted.

He can no longer remain silent. He can no longer pretend as if the disease does not exist.

Instead of going home that night he returns to the laboratory.

By morning the immunologist has formulated the infamous serum that will immunize the city's children against the disease.

On the steps of the Institute before a select group of invited journalists he holds up a vial of his completely colorless serum and explains that he intends to inject it into the bloodstreams of millions and millions of young people. If the municipal authorities have a conscience they will help him do so rather than stand in his way.

But the municipal authorities, and the coalition of industrialists whose interests they represent, have no conscience. To help him immunize the masses against the disease would be to acknowledge the existence of the disease; and to acknowledge the disease now would be to concede that before now they had covered it up. Yet these are clever men, my dear Gretel! They know better than to deny outright the immunologist's entreaty. On the contrary, they affirm their theoretical support for an immunization campaign. They ask "only" for a clearer picture of the nature of the disease and the exact composition of the immunologist's serum.

Such demands, shrewdly contrived to sound as reasonable as possible, are of course never stipulated when it is the children of the rich who are suffering. In that case we do not let children suffer until we have a crystal-clear understanding of the disease! We do not dwell on the chemical niceties of the remedy, so long as the remedy works! No—we act as fast as we can to avert as much suffering as we can. That is our duty as physicians. No, no: first he'll inject his completely colorless serum into the bloodstreams of millions and millions of young people, and then he'll be happy to divulge its composition.

Once his completely colorless serum is circulating in the blood of the masses, immunizing them against a disease the authorities still refuse formally to acknowledge, he will be very happy to divulge its composition.

First it must be in them.

Indefatigably, in specialist and nonspecialist periodicals alike, the immunologist inveighs against the municipal authorities as well as the industrialists whose interests they represent, and lets it be known that our most urgent task is to inject millions and millions of young people with his completely colorless serum.

The authorities neutralize this threat in the customary way. He is called crazy. His key to the Institute is seized from him. His ex-colleagues repudiate his ideas. His friends at the coffeehouse no longer greet him. At home the fact of the disease is not driven out of his head until he drinks twice as much plum brandy as usual. His discussion of morality goes on twice as long, the description of death is twice as detailed. That there is no bedtime kiss no longer surprises him (he refuses to give it that power over him), but when he crawls into bed and feels for his wife's sleeping form he is surprised to find that it is missing. The children are missing, too. He is soon able to confirm his suspicion that everyone dear to him in the world has gone to live with his mother-in-law. In exchange for helping her realize this long-held dream of hers, the immunologist's mother-in-law, while no doubt giddily preparing enormous quantities of her famous goulash, provides the municipal authorities with a pretext for having him committed, in the form of a quote given to a journalist which (inasmuch as it concerns his psychology) is *in principle* unverifiable. The immunologist is informed that it is in his interest to be locked up at the Sanatorium Dr. Krakauer. But of course the only people whose interests are thereby served are the industrialists, who protect their wealth, and his mother-in-law, who gets to look on with quiet joy as her grandchildren consume her goulash, goulash that he, for his part, has always considered undersalted. This victory of the industrialists and of his mother-in-law comes at the expense of the poor, who continue to fall victim en masse to the disease.

Here in the sanatorium the immunologist writes to every member of the coalition of industrialists. He intends to trouble their conscience: What if the children who were dying of this disease happened to be your own?

That question troubles one industrialist, and only one. But it troubles this industrialist enough that he travels all the way to Carinthia to speak with the immunologist in person.

This industrialist is at pains to distinguish himself from all the other industrialists. They are on the right, he is a man of the left. They are warmongers, he is a pacifist. They cling to old hierarchies and the Church, he believes in equality and Science. And so on. He has already given away much of his fortune, and his name even adorns the library in which I now write to you. The industrialist thus exercises considerable influence over Dr. Krakauer, whom he is able to persuade of the immunologist's sanity.

One of his factories for the production of borosilicate glass is converted into a state-of-the-art laboratory where the immunologist produces his serum in industrial quantities.

In a rented hall before the elite of the city the immunologist arranges a public demonstration of the power of the serum.

So as to instill in them an appreciation for the marvels of modern medicine, the industrialist brings along his two children, with whom he sits in the front row.

After introducing his test subjects, a girl and a boy from one of the poor parts of the city, the immunologist announces that as a show of confidence in the power of the serum, his benefactor, the industrialist—a great believer in equality and Science—has asked that his own children be used in their place.

The audience applauds so fervently that the industrialist has no choice but to send his children to the stage.

Which one should be given the injection? the immunologist asks.

The girl, the industrialist replies.

As he injects the completely colorless contents of the syringe into the arm of the industrialist's little girl, the immunologist launches into a long, vituperative, and, to the surprise of the crowd, primarily ethico-political rather than immunological disquisition, the gist of which is that the industrialist who funded the production of this serum is not only no better than all the other industrialists, he is worse. At the end of the disquisition the immunologist declares that the completely colorless serum is now circulating in the little girl's bloodstream and will shortly be entering the chambers of her heart.

Papa? she says.

The industrialist cannot bear to watch what it must now have dawned on him is about to happen. He runs out of the auditorium. Moments later, a gunshot is heard.

It is at this point the immunologist reveals, with a flourish, that the completely colorless serum is nothing more than a simple saline solution! No harm will come to her. In fact, the girl is now fully immunized against the disease. Her brother, too, even though he did not receive the serum, is now fully immunized against the disease. Everyone present, by virtue of witnessing this demonstration, is fully immunized against the disease. And the audience is sufficiently large that the city as a whole is now immune to the disease.

The disease, he explains, is called hypocrisy.

I kiss you good night!

THE JEWELER JUDGES IT UNNECESSARY TO JUMP . . .

For generations his family has festooned the aristocracy. But now the court jeweler is making something for his wife.

He spends long secret nights in his shop's atelier in order to present her with a set of exquisite jewelry on the occasion of the birth of their son.

He works so diligently that even though she goes into labor rather sooner than expected, he succeeds in completing the whole set, apart from the brooch.

But the boy starts to wail when he sees his mother in these jewels and doesn't stop until long after she has torn them off. Never again can he be induced to latch on to her breast.

The distinguished physician summoned to examine the child tells them that his behavior has nothing to do with the jewelry. What we are witnessing unfortunately is something intrinsic to his nature. The course of his life will be a difficult one.

Even though the exquisite jewels are not to blame, the wife cannot be persuaded to put them on again, for it seems obscene to attend to her beauty while her child is suffering. She locks the jewels up and wears the key to the safe on a simple chain round her neck, which even decades later remains her sole adornment.

In that time it becomes clear, albeit for reasons which even the specialists in such matters are unable to determine, that the son cannot bear the presence of his mother. The sight or sound of her sends him into a rage that poses a threat to himself and to those in his vicinity. Even the piano with which she had soothed him when he roiled in the womb now enrages him when he hears her touch it. Early on his parents working in tandem are able to sub-due him at such times. But as he grows into the physical frame of a full-grown man, while retaining the mental capacity of a child, that becomes first difficult and then impossible. Against the coun-sel of every expert the jeweler consults, the wife will not allow the son to be sent to an institution, so he is confined instead to the fifth floor of the family town house, four floors up from the shop that accounts for their wealth and one above the parents whose lives he has brought to grief.

Because she can be neither seen nor heard the jeweler's wife pours her maternal devotion, which without this outlet would have long since overwhelmed her, into the platters of food she lovingly prepares for him three times a day, but which only her husband is permitted to bring to his door, and on which the son leaves everything untouched but the meat. Whole days are spent preparing starches and greens that she must know by now he will never eat, for she clings to the delusion that the abovementioned symptoms of the son's condition are mere foibles he shares with the young men of his time—perhaps heightened by the bewitch-ment that occurred as an infant—and has got it into her head that sending upstairs huge platters of nothing but meat would be tantamount to admitting he is different. The jeweler is well aware that the countless hours spent preparing these starches and greens would be better spent in a thousand other ways, but he knows better than to suggest she forgo them.

In the evenings, when the son is most active, the floorboards creak and groan above their heads, a sound that for the jeweler is soon absorbed into the background hum of life in the city but to which his wife attends closely and from which she claims to deduce the son's movements and mood. "He is stomping the floor in front of the fireplace," she will say, or: "Today he is very upset."

But her interpretations of what the son is up to up there begin to grow baroque, unlikely. "He is circumambulating something of meaning to him, the way the Hindus do . . ." or: "He is thinking about me!" The jeweler fears that after years of bearing her situation as stoically as possible, his wife is now buckling under it. He begs her to take a night off. To do something for herself. At the City Theater, where for twenty years the family box has sat empty, an opera is opening: She should go! The jeweler, who has no ear for music anyhow, will stay home to watch their son.

That evening at the City Theater the jeweler's wife is reborn.

She remembers the existence of a kind of beauty that has nothing to do with one's love for one's child.

The next morning the newspaper informs her that the music that had ravished her was worthless. She reads this review three times. The first time it infuriates her, the second time it intrigues her, and the third time it exhilarates her.

After that she throws herself into the world of symphonies and lieder evenings, of quartets and quintets. In the morning paper she turns first thing to "J. J.," the critic, who impugns in the harshest terms the music that enchanted her evening and prettified her dreams. "The third movement could only have been composed

by someone whose childhood was wholly deprived of sound,"
et cetera. Again and again even the most eminent composers are
accused of having grown up in conditions of absolute silence. Of
having never heard a bell, or a bird. For otherwise their composi-
tions are inexplicable. To the jeweler's wife, the critic's implacable
negativity about all existing music and every actual performance
seems to hold out the promise of an even higher order of beauty.

At a soirée hosted by Holzinger the quarry owner and devoted to
the love songs of Brahms she finally has the pleasure of being in-
troduced to the critic. Far from the old man she had taken him for
from his writing, he is no older than her son. She praises his criti-
cism. He dismisses her praise. He criticizes only to earn money to
compose. But of course he hasn't had a moment to compose since
the day he became a critic. Before that he had been a choirmaster
and then, too, he had not had time to compose. Actually only
in the sanatorium, freed for two years from the basic demands
of everyday life, had he really had time to compose! Now his
operetta-in-progress languishes . . .

In the morning paper Brahms's love songs are attributed to a
childhood deprived of love and song. Brahms as a boy must never
have heard a bird, otherwise his music is inexplicable.

She sees it as her duty to help the young composer complete his
operetta. She tells her husband about him. About his stint as a
choirmaster. The incident that ended it. The spell in an institution.
The simplicity of the operetta he began there at the impetus of his
physician. The way a painful and penurious existence has been
transmuted into a lighthearted farce of mistaken identities and
misplaced (but ultimately requited) passion, set in an idealized
Andalusian village of a prior era. The whitewashed houses that

will span the stage of the City Theater, once the operetta is complete and the General Intendant agrees to produce it. All this is taken as proof of genius by the jeweler's wife, who implores her husband to provide him a stipend. The jeweler cannot help but feel that she is making an invidious comparison between the austerity of the composer's art and the sumptuousness of his own, the purity of the composer's art and the intrinsically transactional nature of his own. Nevertheless, pleased that the ambit of her interests extends beyond the fifth floor of their town house, the jeweler agrees to meet with him. The composer makes a pleasant enough first impression. He asks after the health of the jeweler's son, of whose circumstances he must have been informed in advance. After thanking the composer sincerely for his solicitude, the jeweler, who does not like to discuss this matter with strangers, says only that his son is doing fine, which of course isn't true, and then turns the conversation to the composer's operetta-in-progress. Why Andalusia? But the composer is not finished with his interest in the son's condition. He asks several times for specific details about the young man's behavior—several times: Is he very rambunctious?—and then invites the jeweler to imagine corralling ten, twenty, thirty equally rambunctious boys, forty equally rambunctious boys, even upward of fifty rambunctious boys: Now you know what it is like to be a choirmaster! Imagine being responsible for not just one rambunctious boy but fifty-five of them! And it's not just their health and happiness you are responsible for, you have to make them sing! In harmony! For the glory of God! Ah, the life of a choirmaster! Only now does the composer turn to his operetta-in-progress, naming straight off the sum of money he will need each week to meet the basic demands of everyday life. The sum he names is astronomical. As for Andalusia, he likes the look of the whitewashed walls, that's all, it really could have been set anywhere. Anywhere with such bright white walls.

When the jeweler returns home he notifies his wife that the composer is insane. That no stipend will be provided. That she is neither to see nor to speak of him again.

She receives this pronouncement inscrutably.

Yet the jeweler can find nothing in her subsequent behavior to reproach. She ceases to speak of the young composer. She absents herself from the musical scene so as not to bump into him by mistake. She even alters her attitude toward their son, forgoing the self-deluding dinners that had once taken up all of her time and instead sticking an animal in the oven three days a week. Once or twice he hears her mutter "It is hopeless," which, inasmuch as it implies a view of the son's condition that accords at last with reality, gives the jeweler grounds, paradoxically, for hope.

He is moved to do something he has not done in a long time: To make his wife a piece of jewelry. To complete the set that his son's premature arrival had left undone. He will make his wife a brooch.

Once again he spends long secret nights in the atelier. But this time is different. Because this time he knows what she likes. This time he feels he is making something for *her*. He now understands, for example, that that simple chain with that little key has spent all these years around his wife's neck only because the plainness of it agrees with her taste. He will make a brooch to match.

The brooch is like nothing he has ever made before. He is immediately aware that there is something magical about the brooch. That the brooch is bound to bring his wife happiness.

When, however, he presents her with that simple white brooch and pins it to the throat of her dress, he notices that the chain it was supposed to match is missing. He suspects that he knows why. And when, to his suggestion that she go try on the full set, she quietly replies that that is no longer possible, he knows that his suspicions are correct. That everything has been pawned. For the furtherance of the composer's operetta.

The jeweler surprises himself by wrapping his hands round her neck and squeezing the life out of her. But when she falls to the floor he admits to himself that a part of him has always known this would happen, or something like it.

Just then, across the square, he sees the youngest Princess at her window with a strange look on her face. She must have seen everything. He therefore throws open his window and leans almost all the way out. But the jeweler realizes that he is not ready to die. And so he tells himself: The Princess is not looking at you, she's looking slightly beneath you, at the flowerbox. It is not you that fascinates her, it's the flowers! And by telling himself this he justifies closing the window. That night he waits till the floorboards stop creaking and groaning. Then he hauls his wife's body up to the fifth floor. In the morning he summons the police, who chalk it up as a case of a mother who simply could not go another day without seeing her severely disturbed child, even in full cognizance of what an encounter with him would mean.

As far as the authorities are concerned, it was always only a matter of time before they were called to take the son away. Their only surprise, really, was the brooch he was modeling for them when they arrived, which, he told them, made him feel, for the first time, handsome. He had never thought of himself as a handsome person; but then, he had never worn such a brooch. With this tasteful and not at all overdone brooch, he finally felt on par with his peers. For reasons he had never understood his parents had always found him difficult to live with, but with this brooch he knew he would have no trouble making his way in the world. This beautiful brooch, which was the last thing his beloved mother ever gave him, was impossible to look away from, he said, and not even in court, as the judge ruled that he was perfectly sane and so sentenced him to die, did the jeweler's son take his eyes off it for a moment.

I kiss you good night!

K

THE KINDERGARTEN TEACHER CAN NO LONGER KOW-
TOW TO THE CURRICULUM . . .

She leads the children into the woods behind the schoolhouse in
order to acquaint them firsthand with the plants that grow there
and the animals that live there.

This is something the headmaster has, in the past, expressly
forbidden.

Whenever she sought his permission to lead the children into
the woods, he asked her, please, to stick to the curriculum. The
woods were no place for small children.

So she never led them into the woods. Really, she only wants
what is best for them. She has long since made peace with her
spinsterhood and has come to think of the children in her charge
as her own, or almost her own.

But when the class begins the unit on plants and animals, the headmaster's interdiction against bringing the children into the woods
begins to strike her as not only wrong but unconscionable.

How can she make them recite such banalities as *The hare hops,
the boar grunts, the stag leaps* or *The roots spread, the leaves fall,
the trees grow straight and tall* when in the vast woods they can

see from their classroom window actual hares, boars, and stags doubtless run among the roots, leaves, and trees?

Learning must start from sense impressions, and only then proceed to concepts, but this curriculum hurls the child straightaway into an airless world of ungrounded abstraction!

She must lead the children into the woods, she must show them the plants and animals.

Yet with the meekness that has marked her nature even to this point in her life, she seeks, as always, the headmaster's permission.

If she is under the illusion that their having commenced the unit on plants and animals might soften his stance on their entering the woods, he disabuses her of that notion right away. Please adhere to the curriculum! The woods are no place for small children! Then the headmaster mutters something the kindergarten teacher will not be able to understand until later: And as far as the unit on plants and animals is concerned, those woods are half-useless anyway . . .

There is nothing the kindergarten teacher wants more in the world than to lead these thirty children whom she thinks of almost as her own into the woods to show them the plants and animals, but it is not in her nature to flout the order of an authority figure.

However, something now occurs in the kindergarten teacher's private life to alter that nature. Her sister, the famous ballerina, who had been blessed with a child even though—her body being her means of expression—she had never wanted one, falls off the stage at the City Theater and dies. The kindergarten teacher is not present at this performance, for she was never invited to such things, and would not have gone even if she had been. But the sound of her celebrated sister's skull striking the edge of the kettledrum is described so vividly in the morning paper that she can hear it reverberating in her own head.

It awakens her from a long bewitchment. She is strong now, she is no longer meek.

At that moment she resolves to lead the children into the woods with or without the headmaster's sanction.

She furnishes each child with a crisp red apple and bids them to follow her, first silently, as they pass by the headmaster's office, and then, upon entering the woods, with as much rambunctious-ness as their lively little bodies desire. The children laugh and sing, they toss their apples high into the air and catch them again. The kindergarten teacher shows them roots spreading, leaves falling, trees growing straight and tall, and urges them to keep their ears open and their eyes peeled for hares, boars, and stags.

After several hours, however, they have not seen a single animal.

By now the children are dragging their feet. One has disclosed a wish to go home. But it is her duty as their teacher to know them better than they know themselves. And she knows that with the sight of a boar or a stag, or even a hare, their fatigue will van-ish and they will feel nothing but joy. She therefore explains that the noise and bustle of the big city must have pushed these poor creatures deeper and deeper into the woods, and so to set eyes on them they shall have to go just a little deeper themselves.

But by the time darkness starts to fall they still haven't seen a single hopping hare, not a single grunting boar or leaping stag. There are times when she thinks she sees something moving among the trees, but it is never a boar, it is never a stag, it is always only one of the children. Any grunting she hears is only the grunting or the sobbing of a child. Now it is dark and drizzly, the children are shivering, their apples are long gone. The kindergarten teacher recalls the words of the headmaster: As far as the unit on plants and animals is concerned, these woods are half-useless anyway . . .

She feels an urge to tell the children what she now knows to be true—that the woods are lifeless, that this lifelessness appalls, and betokens something sinister—but she restricts herself to telling them that they have seen a lot of wonderful plants that day and some really impressive root systems, but they'd have to save the animals for next time.

They turn back.

But she becomes uncertain of the way. This, she feels, is not how they came. Before long it is pitch black. The children are hungry and thirsty, soaked through and chilled to the bone. So it is true: The woods are no place for small children. Though the kindergarten teacher drives them frantically forward, they cannot take another step, they fall where they stand. She lies down among them, takes off everything but her undergarments to cover them with, and draws them all near her body to comfort them and keep them warm. They lie like this in silence awhile. In the darkness she feels thirty small bodies breathing in and out all around her own, she can feel their heartbeats and they can surely feel hers, and she cannot dispel the suspicion that at this moment she and they are strangely content. That in the midst of their terror she and the children have found intimacy and bliss. That there is nowhere else any of them would rather be.

Just then, with one voice, all the children cry out for their mothers.

They want to see their mothers: of course they do. Probably all day long they had been wanting to see their mothers, not the trees, not the leaves, their mothers. Not the root systems, their mothers. Not the animals she had been so desperate to show them, their mothers. Nothing can substitute for mothers, not even fathers, let alone boars. But of course she can no more show them their mothers than she'd been able to show them the animals. *You are stuck with me!* cries the kindergarten teacher. The children cease their bawling. Then, contrite, and seized by the realization that if she cannot lead the children out of the woods it will fall to her to help them die in it, she adds, more gently: We, my dears, are the only beings here.

No sooner has she said this than the beam of a torch falls on them and a familiar voice says: Come with me.

The kindergarten teacher covers herself with her hands. Who's there? Is that the headmaster?

The headmaster? The man laughs a familiar laugh. No, he says. It's not the headmaster.

Then who are you?

Who are *you*? Are you aware that you're trespassing in the ducal game preserve? You're lucky that I and not one of my men came across you. But it is too late now to show you the way out. You will have to spend the night in the lodge. Come along, bring the thirty children. Or stay here, and good luck to you! There'll be a frost tonight.

His beam swings around the other way and moves off swiftly into the woods. In all her years on the outskirts of the city, at the edge of the woods, the kindergarten teacher has never heard anyone speak of a ducal game preserve. That is not what disturbs her most, though. If the man had said, *Bring the children*, she would have followed him without a second thought. But *Bring the thirty children* was unnerving. It did not seem possible to count them all so quickly and accurately in the dark, all heaped together as they were.

The children, however, tug at her hands, her hair, her skin, they want to go with him, and his beam of light is growing fainter and fainter. And it's true at least what he said about the frost, the rain has already turned almost to sleet . . .

She throws on her clothes and cries: Come, children!

And they all run after the man.

In time he leads them to a simple little cabin. The lodge, he calls it. Welcome.

It has two small rooms and a fire going, by the light of which she can see the man clearly. He has a coiled horn on a strap around his neck, a green felt hat on his big blond head, and a long stick in one hand. So, he really isn't the headmaster. He points his stick at one of the rooms and tells the children: You're in here. There's stew on the table. Eat your fill and go to sleep. Then he points at the other room and tells the kindergarten teacher: We'll have a drink or two in here.

She says: I would like to stay with the children.

We'll have a drink or two in here, put some color back in your skin, and then you can do as you please, he says, escorting her into the other room. He shuts the door, pulls a chair in front of it, and sits down. Then he leans over and pats the foot of the bed. Have a seat. The bed is all hers tonight. Don't worry about him, he won't sleep, the forest keeps him up. The problems of forest management . . .

She is strong now, she is no longer meek, she does not have to do what he says. So as she sits on the bed she knows that a part of her must want to do so. He pours two glasses of schnapps and hands her one. The kindergarten teacher can't remember the last time she had a drink with a man. She sniffs at the liquid. He drains his glass and pours himself another. In the next room, past the man and his stick, on the other side of the door, she hears the chatter of the children and the clink and scrape of their spoons on the pot.

Drink up, the man says. It'll warm you.

As she brings the glass to her lips she takes the opportunity to glance around, first at the man's face, as if to remind herself that he is not the headmaster whose voice his own so closely resembles, and then upward at the bare white walls.

What? he says. What is it? What do you notice?

Nothing, she says. It's very nice. I've never been in a duke's hunting lodge before. Only I might have expected perhaps some antlers on the wall . . .

A duke's hunting lodge!

The man roars with laughter.

You think this is the Duke's hunting lodge? Then you must think I am the Duke? Or—aha, now I understand! You think *I* think I'm the Duke! Yes: *You* think *I* think I am the Duke! You think you and your thirty children have fallen into the hands of a madman! You think: He takes his little hut for a hunting lodge, himself for a duke, and God only knows what he put in that stew!

More laughter.

No, no, I am not the Duke. And this is not the Duke's hunting lodge. However, he says, draining the second glass of schnapps and pouring himself a third, the Duke's hunting lodge is but a hundred paces that way. You would see it clear as day through that window right there if the night were not so dark. As it is, of course, you see nothing. But trust that it is there, that it is for-midable, and that its walls inside are festooned with hundreds of heads and horns, so much so that the narrower hallways can be navigated only with difficulty and the smaller rooms are no lon-ger fit for human habitation. I hope that accords better with your expectations? No, my dear lady, *this* is only the gamekeeper's lodge. I am the head gamekeeper. It is my duty to ensure that the forest at all times is amply stocked with game.

The man drains the third glass and pours himself a fourth.

The kindergarten teacher listens for the chattering of the children, the clinking and scraping. She no longer hears it. The other room has fallen silent. She has a mind to lunge for the door. But the man holds up his stick like a staff.

Rest, my dear lady, rest! the man says. Rest. All is well. The children have finished their stew and fallen asleep by the warmth of the fire. They were exhausted, that was clear to see. And you must be exhausted, too. You may sip your schnapps lying down if you'd like.

I should check on them.

The door that stands between you and them creaks terribly, it would wake them up. And once one has woken up in an unfamiliar place it is never easy to fall back asleep. Let them sleep. They've had a very long day, they are warm now, their bellies are full. Let them sleep. They are beautiful children! Of course all children are beautiful, but I think these thirty especially so. Sip your schnapps lying down, it's fine if you spill a little.

What did you put in the stew?

The stew was a standard stew, my dear lady! A standard stew. What I said earlier was only a poor attempt at humor. (He puts his hat over his heart.) Word of honor, it's a standard stew. Out here in the forest I don't often have the chance to see children, I had forgotten how beautiful they can be. It was a privilege to feed them. Do you have any children of your own?

No.

No? How come? An attractive woman such as yourself? Well, my wife never conceived, either. And some of what's gone on here in this forest has persuaded me it's for the best. It is in the best interest of some children not to be conceived. Lie down and I'll tell you. It all comes back to the question of forest management, lie down, I'll tell you, it's fine if you spill a little. Lie down, lie down! She's strong now, she's no longer meek, so perhaps a part of her wants to do so, since it takes only the gentlest touch from the man's stick to guide her down till she is flat on her back. He begins: I don't know how much you know about forest management. But it cannot have escaped you that this forest is not healthy. There is something wrong with it. What did you notice was wrong?

Nothing, it's very nice.

My dear lady, there is nothing you can possibly say about this forest that I haven't said myself ten thousand times over, and more savagely than you could ever put it! What's wrong with the forest?

There are no animals in it.

There are no animals in it. There is not a single animal in it. This forest is bereft of life. But it wasn't always so. In fact, many years ago, when the Duke was deciding where to build his hunting lodge, he selected this forest precisely for its abundance of hares, boars, and stags . . .

The hunting lodge had been the Duke's gift to his bride. The Duke himself found hunting grotesque, but the Duchess-to-be had grown up hunting with her father, so the Duke built this lodge for her on the sly and hired the man and his brother to ensure a steady supply of game. When, however, on the eve of their wedding, the Duke unveiled it, his bride burst into tears. She hated her father. Her wedding was supposed to mark the end of that part of her life in which she had to feign an interest in the hunt. When the Duke was told the cause of her tears he embraced her and told her that if it was her wish, no rifle would ever be fired on these grounds. This could be a place where animals were left in peace. Where animals could flourish. That pleased her. And in the course of the following year she came often to walk among the hares and boars and feed the stags apples from her hand. Only when the Duchess fell pregnant did she stop coming, for her doctors advised her that wild creatures like these carry invisible organisms that can affect the brain of the fetus. That sounded outlandish to the two gamekeepers, whose mother had spent her whole life around animals, as had their mother's mother. These fancy doctors are constantly coming up with new invisible organisms to justify their existence and extend their dominion, it's no coincidence they're all Jews. Still, the brothers grew nervous as the ninth month approached. Even if something *did* happen to the brain of the child they could hardly be held responsible, for it was the Duchess who chose to be so affectionate with the stags. They were frightened anyway. What a relief to be told that the Duchess had given birth to a healthy baby girl!

A few months later the Duchess showed up. She said: I need one day without my daughter. They gave her a sack of apples to feed the stags. But she wasn't interested in that. She wanted to kill something, she said. The man brought her a rifle and his brother took her to the blind. There she explained herself the same way as before: I need one day without my daughter. She didn't leave the blind until nightfall, by which time she had shot three hares, two boars, and a stag. They thought she would be pleased. Instead she was irate. When she went hunting with her father the animals had run back and forth before them in vast numbers all day long. They'd never gone home before shooting at least a dozen beasts each. How poorly these two must be managing the forest!

The brothers looked at each other. The Duchess's father had obviously had the animals driven before them by beaters; was it really conceivable that the Duchess didn't know that? Had her father let her think that was nature's doing? That all day long the animals ran of their own volition toward the guns? He must've kept hidden from her the brutal mechanics of it. The brothers knew at once that they ought to do the same. They went to the Duke and asked permission to hire a team of beaters. The Duke found driven hunts particularly abhorrent. But he wanted his wife to be happy again. He gave them permission to hire beaters. After that the Duchess did not return for some time. She had fallen pregnant again. Then one day she showed up and demanded a gun. I hope you've been managing the forest better than before, she said. They brought her to the blind and then blew the horn. The beaters thwacked the trees with their sticks till the animals were flushed out into the clearing before the Duchess. She shot them down. Then, taking care not to be seen by her, the beaters circled around to the other side, waited for the next blast of the horn, and then drove the animals the other way, the man told the kindergarten teacher, swishing his own stick in the air. By nightfall the clearing was littered with hundreds of dead boars and stags and the carcasses of countless hares. I needed this, the Duchess said as she examined the carnage by the light of a torch: I needed one day without my daughters.

It was fortunate that she did not return for another year, as it took nearly that long to restore the forest to its former condition. The brothers planted grasses and trees, dammed up streams to form watering holes, concealed rutting areas behind thickets of brush. At night they patrolled for poachers. For a year they did not sleep. But by the end of that year they had replenished the supply of game. Then the Duchess came back, three months postpartum. She took her rifle to the blind and decimated the animal population in an afternoon. I am allowed, she said, to have one day without my daughters. So it went, year after year. A year's worth of ceaseless forest management undone in a day. And every year it got harder, because the animals bred with greater reluctance, no matter how thickly the brothers concealed their rutting areas. It had nothing to do with the rutting areas: they seemed to know the fate of their young ones. One day the brother returned from one of the rutting areas reporting that as crazy as it sounded he was now certain the animals were aware that their lives were governed by the Duchess's maternal-psychological cycles. There seemed to be some truth in this. But after that the man realized he'd have to keep an eye on his brother. Each year the supply of game diminished. The Duchess had ever more pointed words for their methods of forest management. The forest's only hope was that she would stop having children. But she did not stop. Three, four, five, six. All of them girls. The gamekeeper's wife had always wanted a little girl, just one. But she never conceived, he told the kindergarten teacher, draining his fourth glass of schnapps and pouring himself a fifth. She put their failure to conceive at the foot of the Duchess. It wasn't just that he was always working. She had developed a theory according to which the Duchess had "sponged up" the fecundity of the whole forest. His fecundity, hers, and that of the animals. She pointed out that the forest had been a profoundly fecund place when the Duchess, then childless, first set foot in it. Now it was barren, while the Duchess was propagating at an incredible rate. She must have sponged up the forest's fecundity. His wife did not pretend to know how.

Now he had to keep an eye on his wife as well. She spent her days in bed deciphering the signs of her own body. Meanwhile his brother concealed the rutting areas ever more thickly without believing that that would accomplish anything. The gamekeeper realized that he himself was the only person in the whole forest who was not going mad.

By the time the Duchess had seven daughters, there were only two little boars left. The hunting horn blew, the beaters thwacked the trees, the first little boar ran into the clearing, and the Duchess shot it dead. Then the other little boar emerged. But something strange happened. The man's brother emerged also, positioned himself between the boar and the blind, and escorted the animal like that all the way across the clearing. When the horn blew a second time and the boar was driven the other way, the man's brother did the same thing again. The Duchess summoned the man to the blind and ordered him to restrain his brother. When the horn blew a third time the boar came into the clearing alone and the Duchess shot it dead. She summoned the man back to the blind.

Where are the other animals?

Madam, there are no other animals.

Then we shall have to find another way to entertain ourselves! she said, seizing his hand.

As soon as they had finished it became clear that he had been used for her own purposes, for she lay down on the floor and elevated her hips. My husband, she said, is capable only of producing girls. After a quarter of an hour the Duchess got up and left. Since then she has not returned. Nor have the papers reported any royal births. Meanwhile his brother and wife finally lost their minds completely. His brother walked out of the forest, his wife walked deeper into it. Both had gone in search of "new life" and just had different ideas about where it could be found. She disappeared, he went into elementary school administration and what is called curricular development. There, I presume, is your *headmaster*, the gamekeeper says with a laugh. I myself remain committed to the forest, I still believe it is possible to bring life back into it. And I mean to do so. For I am not convinced that the Duchess is done with this place. There are times when I pass by the blind and feel virtually certain that she is in there with her gun. One day she'll summon me again. But first I must supply her with beasts. That is only fair. It's a question of forest management, the gamekeeper tells the kindergarten teacher, draining his sixth schnapps and placing the glass on the floor.

The next morning the sun is shining, the children are rested, and through the window the kindergarten teacher can see the formidable hunting lodge the gamekeeper had sworn would be there.

He brings them to the path that will lead them out of the forest. In high spirits they wave goodbye and make their way along it.

They have gone a little ways when the kindergarten teacher is suddenly moved to rise up on one foot and do a little pirouette. The children laugh and clap. She hasn't done that in a long time, probably since she was a girl! Back then her pirouettes were better than her sister's, faster, cleaner, their teacher always said so. She does another one, but the instant she lands, before the children can bring their hands together, they hear the blast of a horn. There is motion in the trees behind them, and then the thwack of wood against wood.

The children start to run.

The kindergarten teacher realizes what is happening.

Stop! she cries. Children, stop!

But they don't listen to her. They don't stop.

Please, children, stop!

They don't listen to her. If she were their mother, they would listen to her. But she isn't their mother, they don't listen to her.

They come out into a clearing and keep running. There ahead of them is the blind. They run straight toward it. Is that a face in the window? Stop, children, stop! But why should they listen? She's not their mother. They don't have to listen to her, she's not their mother!

Any moment now she expects to hear the first gunshot.

Yet it doesn't come.

And why would a hunting blind have flowerboxes? The children run up to it and peek inside. So does she. It's no blind at all, it's just an old mill. And no one's in there, only some derelict furniture and a few buckets of paint. The gamekeeper runs up to them. He's sorry for startling them, he only wanted to get their attention. They have taken a wrong turn. He shows them the right way and says goodbye again.

Finally the class emerges from the forest. The parents, weeping in the schoolhouse, are first inexpressibly relieved and then unappeasably furious. But their children lack the means to describe what has happened to them. Their accounts are so confused and contradictory that the headmaster must inform their parents that there are no grounds on which to punish their teacher. Nor, in truth, does he want to punish her. He wants to embrace her, and to articulate at last the feelings he has always felt for her. He welcomes her thoughts on the curriculum—she's right, it ought to start from sensation! And just like that, the kindergarten teacher's life as a spinster is over. When a child arrives the headmaster is able to determine by elementary arithmetic that she cannot be his, but he resolves never to tell the girl so, nor to ask her mother what happened in the woods.

Good night!

THE LIGHTING TECHNICIAN ILLUMINATES THE LIEUTEN-
ANT'S DAUGHTER . . .

He arrives at the City Theater with high hopes of forming warm friendships with both the company and the crew.

This is a task he sets about with care, for in his youth he had often blundered in the first few sentences he exchanged with a new person. And because of that blunder someone who by every metric might have been perfectly suited to become an intimate friend remained, instead, a stranger, or became an enemy. In his ignorance of the art of conversation he not only failed to win people over but even arrayed them against him.

It was in order to rectify that ignorance that he was drawn to the theater. This development scandalized his guardians. He had excelled in his studies at the Polytechnic Institute. A lucrative career awaited him in a factory for the production of borosilicate glassware. Instead he went into the theater. For, as he explained to his guardians in the note with which he bid them farewell, if one wishes to comprehend the nature of human interaction—the various stratagems by which one individual secures the interest and affection of another—then even the most provincial theater is a world-class laboratory.

If his guardians wanted someone to blame, they, who raised him in seclusion from other children and were therefore responsible for his infelicities with them, should look only to themselves.

From the high perch from which he operated the limelight he had an incomparable view of the men and women onstage engaged in the age-old struggle of nurturing in one another's breast a feeling of fondness and devotion. The actors addressed one another and reacted to one another, and over time he learned which sentences had which effects. What produced a grimace, what produced a smile. What produced a laugh! What produced tears, and what produced no effect.

In light of these observations it pains the lighting technician to recall the conversations of his youth. How oblivious he had been! How naive! For he sees now that the things he thought would produce smiles were precisely those that produce no effect, and the things he thought would produce laughter were also those that produce no effect.

On account of his outstanding technical proficiency the lighting technician rises in time from a distant provincial theater to the very center of the dramatic world, the City Theater itself.

By now he has witnessed thousands or tens of thousands of human interactions, indeed many more than even an ordinary childhood would have enabled him to see, and he is ready to put into practice all that he has gleaned in order to form warm friendships with the company and the crew.

He strikes up a conversation with this or that actor or stagehand. First he introduces himself. He gives his name—which, imagine, is something he'd often failed to do in his youth!—and notes that he is the new lighting technician. He offers pleasantries, a witticism, and praise for a recent action his interlocutor has performed. Then he touches briefly on the role of stage lighting in the theater, because the art of theater is a topic that binds all of them together and is therefore a topic of common interest and common concern. Here, or shortly thereafter, he brings the conversation to a prompt conclusion, because he knows that as a young man he more than once allowed a conversation to go past the point at which it should have been curtailed.

After these introductory conversations, the lighting technician manages to suss out from his high perch the particular interests of his new acquaintances and adapts himself to them, since friendships are very often solidified in this manner. He is always happy to discuss with any of the actors all of the reasons their characters act the way they do. With the crew, who enjoy discussing food and drink, money, wives, and mothers-in-law, the exploits of their adolescence, the ducal family, and the perfidiousness of the Slavs, the lighting technician makes himself available to discuss any and all of these matters. Every now and then, only so as not to seem like someone without interests of his own, he makes mention of the role of stage lighting in the theater.

One day he overhears several actors and stagehands discussing that very topic. One suggests that lighting in the theater is not merely a matter of letting the audience see what is happening onstage; it can also serve as its own means of expression. The lighting technician hastens to join this conversation, since these are views to which he is immensely sympathetic! But it dawns on him, too slowly, that they are only reciting a conversation he himself had initiated in the past. Of course in this rendition the conversation is given a comic spin . . . Somehow, despite all of his precautions, he has developed a reputation as someone who is always going around propounding at length a theory of stage lighting . . .

In short, he has blundered!

From then on the lighting technician converses with no one. He does his work but holds his tongue. He resigns himself to the reality that he is not one of those people destined to enjoy the pleasures of friendship, since he has nothing to tell anyone that they wish to hear. The things he knows are of interest to no one but himself.

His only companion—she cannot be called a friend—is the General Intendant's daughter, because with her he feels under no obligation to speak.

Presently a new play, *The Lieutenant's Daughter*, goes into production at the City Theater.

The General Intendant, who commissioned the play, is codirecting it, and has cast his daughter in the title role, instructs the lighting technician to increase the brightness of the limelight that shines on her during the scene of her interrogation. The lighting technician does so. The General Intendant wants it even brighter. The lighting technician increases the brightness as much as present technology permits. Yet even this is not bright enough for the General Intendant, who now takes the lighting technician aside to impress upon him the importance of this scene:

The lieutenant, a highly decorated officer, is suspected of peddling state secrets in order to finance a morally repugnant habit. Agents of the state, who have reason to believe that his daughter, a pious individual, knows of his habit, and abominates it, subject her to interrogation in a cell richly (if somewhat ineptly) ornamented with Catholic iconography. It is suggested, without their or the script's saying so outright, that the excruciatingly bright light they shine in her eyes is nothing less than the Divine Light itself, which will reveal the contents of her soul whether or not she chooses to voice them. By staging a confrontation between the lieutenant's daughter and her own religiously hypertrophied conscience, they seem to imagine that they will bring the interrogation to a swift and satisfactory conclusion. But the daughter does not say a word. Even as the agents assail her with details about her father's repugnant habit, some of them probably based in truth, others invented from whole cloth, she says nothing. The agents come to realize that the lieutenant's daughter—who for reasons the script doesn't touch upon is confined to a wheelchair—cannot be brought to reveal anything. She obviously knows everything but will reveal nothing. The strength of this woman, and of her love for her father, is impossible to comprehend in secular terms. They give up. They turn off the light. At that moment, in the dark, the daughter emits an almost primordial sound. She cannot abide the dark. It was only in the bright light (with which they thought they were intimidating her!) that she found the courage to hold her tongue. We are not party to her ensuing disclosures, the scene ends with the primordial sound, her ensuing disclosures are implied. The next scene confirms that she must have revealed everything the state needed to know, for the lieutenant (played by Silberberg, the eminent actor and tenor) is arrested. End of Act II.

So you see, concludes the General Intendant: the limelight will have to be considerably brighter.

The lighting technician tries replacing the quicklime with magnesium, then the magnesium with zirconium. The magnesium burns brighter than the quicklime, the zirconium brighter than the magnesium. But neither of them burns bright enough for the General Intendant, nothing burns bright enough for the General Intendant. He hounds the lighting technician: Brighter! Brighter! Brighter! The lighting technician racks his brain. Then he dimly recalls a substance he learned about in school. For the first time in many years, the lighting technician writes to his former guardians. He asks them to send him his notes from the Polytechnical Institute. In order not to give them the wrong impression, or false hope, he adds as a postscript: This is all in service of the performing arts. In these notes he finds a single line on the substance in question: *First discovered by miners in J——, first described by Prof. O. Mayrhofer, has remarkable incandescent properties, though inimical to human life if handled improperly.*

The lighting technician obtains this substance and swaps it for the zirconium. The light it emits when burned is bright enough to satisfy at last the General Intendant.

Yet another of its incandescent properties is even more remarkable: namely, that the surface of the stage, which to the naked eye or in ordinary limelight had seemed immaculate and polished to a sheen, is revealed in this light to be stained in many places by what are unmistakably the traces of a crime.

Wherever the lighting technician shines the light from his high perch he brings forth traces of the crime. There is hardly a corner of the City Theater untouched by this crime, from the stage to the stalls, the aisles to the exits. That can only mean that the victim—or victims—of this crime, whatever it was, did not go down easily but rather ran hither and thither, banging on this or that door, trying every conceivable means of escape, until their pursuer caught them at last and life leaked out of them completely.

When his amazement subsides the lighting technician is overtaken by joy, because he has observed time and time again that people from all walks of life like nothing more than to speculate about a crime.

Now that he knows something of interest to others he comes down from his high perch to share it with them. By the exit where the traces of the crime are most vivid, and where therefore he has trained his new spotlight, he awaits one or another of the company or crew. He greets them with pleasantries and a witticism, states his name again in case they've forgotten it, and then indicates the monstrous crime that must have occurred at their feet.

However, years of isolation have taken their toll. The lighting technician swallows his words, they cannot understand him. They seem to think he is showing them the light itself, rather than the traces of the crime the light discloses. They seem to think he is propounding a theory of stage lighting, when nothing could be further from the truth!

Only the General Intendant's daughter takes the time to examine the traces with him. To her alone he offers his speculations about who committed the crime, against whom, and for what reason. But this cannot be called a friendship.

The night of the premiere arrives.

The curtain rises at the City Theater.

The first act is a triumph. But in the second act, in the second-to-last scene, as the agents of the state conduct their interrogation, the blindingly bright spotlight strays from the lieutenant's daughter in order to illuminate a part of the set which (though it has been covered up with Catholic iconography) is still clearly stained by traces of the crime. The audience gasps. So, they see it! At that moment the lighting technician feels at one with them and with the world. Then it dawns on him they are not gasping for the right reason, it's not because they see traces of a crime, it's because that part of the set is now on fire. Now the primordial sound is emitted. An instant later the whole theater goes up in flames. Because the exits open inward, multitudes die. But because the company and crew have access to the stage door, all of them survive. The only exceptions are the General Intendant's daughter, immobile onstage in her cane-backed wheelchair, and her father, who is last seen running toward her.

The fire is declared an accident. Nevertheless, the lighting technician considers it in his own best interest to have himself committed to the Sanatorium Dr. Krakauer. What disturbs him most about his own state of mind is that his speculations about the crime proved one hundred percent correct.

Here at the sanatorium his fortunes take a turn.

First Klamt, the famous former starlet, upon learning that this was the man who burned down the City Theater, takes his face in her hands and plants a kiss on his forehead.

Then, from an audience member who survived the fire, he receives a letter congratulating him on the brightness he achieved with his lighting. This audience member was composing an operetta set in an old Andalusian village, but none of the methods of stage lighting known to him were capable of conveying the blinding whiteness of its walls. The letter ends with the audience member's address and an invitation to visit as soon as the lighting technician leaves the institution.

After a lifetime of no friends, he suddenly has two! However, a man capable of forming friendships, capable of forming two friendships, hardly needs to be here. The lighting technician committed himself voluntarily; he is free to leave at any time. Dr. Krakauer urges him to stay a little while longer. But he will do no such thing, the lighting technician thinks as he folds up the composer's letter and puts it carefully in his pocket.

I kiss you good night!

M

THE MOTHER MISSES MUSIC . . .

So as soon as the child is weaned she begins taking singing lessons. First an hour a week, then an hour and a half. The child wails when she walks out the door: Mama! Mama! The father hushes the child because he knows this time is important to the mother. For an hour each week she is not just a mother, she's a mezzo-soprano! Then the length of time for which she's a mezzo, not a mother, is extended to the aforementioned hour and a half, not counting the time it takes to get there and back. She comes home dizzy with the Maestro's praise. One day she will sing onstage, he says! The father is no musician. Still, he has ears to hear: he is well aware that this praise is in outrageous disproportion to her voice. Thus the Maestro's intentions become clear. Of course, he cannot say so. He can say so to the child but not to the mother. He restricts himself to observing that it is difficult these days to get anything onstage. Then it is two hours twice a week for which she is a mezzo, not a mother. In other words four hours each week she is no mother. Not counting the time it takes to get there and back. Though the child wails he no longer hushes her because he feels in his heart that she is right to protest. Mama! Mama! He says nothing. She's not wrong to protest. One evening when the mother is hours late coming home from a recital the father, operating on the principle that children always understand everything anyway, tells the child the truth. That motherhood is an insufficient justification for the mother's existence. That the mother finds herself ill-suited for the role and cannot help but blame the two of them for casting her in it. That the Maestro, meanwhile, is exploit-ing all this for his own evil ends. That under the circumstances it is in everyone's interest to let her go without guilt into the world where she thinks she belongs. But that the delusion that she has something inside of her that needs to be expressed will never-theless destroy her life and theirs. Now the mother saunters up the road. In her hands she holds a loose wreath formed from the flowers strewn at her feet, with which she presumably intends to crown the child. By this ploy she hopes to deflect attention from what took place after the recital, even though what took place is attested to by each of her shining features and is legible even in the self-conscious positioning of her limbs. As she unlocks the front door she cannot keep her joy in check. Gretel! Gretel! First she sings it, then she simply calls it out. Finally she screams it. But of course you were no longer there.

THE NEUROLOGIST KNOWS THAT THE NATURALIST MUST HAVE REDUCED HIS DAUGHTER TO NOTHING . . .

The naturalist returns from the far north with innumerable speci-
mens of rare and beautiful birds, which it is his highest aspiration
to display in the hallowed cases of the Natural History Museum.
He skins and stuffs bird after bird. Yet the museum declines every
one of them. It gives no reasons, but none are needed, the truth is
plain to see: The birds have no life in them. He has failed to im-
bue them with the spirit of living things. The problem is his little
girl, for whom, with her mother gone and her French governess
dismissed, the naturalist suddenly finds himself solely responsible. He loves his daughter, that goes without saying. But her exu-
berance makes taxidermy difficult. Her laughter, her squeals, her
constant questions about the meanings of things: it gladdens his
heart but destroys the conditions necessary for taxidermy. Therefore, as he prepares to skin and stuff the very last of his birds, a
large heron with white plumage, he enjoins her to be quiet. After
that it is possible to concentrate. The heron is a tricky bird to
mount, on account of its long, kinked neck in which the vertebrae
are visible. It takes him a while. But he produces in the end a marvelously animated bird, its neck tensely coiled as if on the verge
of spearing a fish. He feels at last that he has made something
with life in it. When, however, he takes his daughter's hands for a
celebratory waltz he realizes that besides being all grown up now
and nearly as tall as he, she has been struck dumb in the interim.
She no longer laughs, squeals, or speaks. She keeps silent and

stares straight ahead. It is clear what has happened: All the qualities that made his little girl a living being have been absorbed by the heron. That can be seen, for example, in the heron's neck. He weeps about it, but the naturalist knows that his tears are an indulgence, for what's done is done. He removes the red ribbons from her hair and finds a place for her where her silence will not seem out of place. Then he sets out to honor her: to honor her by honoring the heron. He brings the heron to the Natural History Museum, where it is acquired at once and mounted posthaste in the Hall of Birds . . .

All of the foregoing is deduced by a certain museumgoer, a neurologist by trade.

He deduces it all from close inspection of the stuffed white heron.

As a boy the neurologist had frequented the Natural History Museum, and especially the Hall of Birds, because his mother thought it important for a child to know about the natural world, in which birds obviously play a not insignificant part. Of late he has been frequenting it again, because in his mother's dementia it was the only place where her agitation was stilled. Everywhere else she still tried to formulate words and sentences, with all the distress that entailed. But here among the birds she was content to clutch his hand and sit in silence.

The white heron, in particular, brought her peace.

In the final stretch of her illness his colleagues were wholly understanding about his prolonged leave of absence from the Pathological-Anatomical Institute. She, after all, had no one else. And he, a lifelong bachelor, had no one else either. Yet one, two, even three months after her death, his laboratory there remains locked and shuttered. Still they say nothing. At least not to him. It can well be imagined, though, that among themselves they have begun to grumble or speculate. The neurologist therefore explains himself by posting a placard in one of the Institute's communal spaces which states that the answers to the questions neurologists like to pose are as likely to be found in the Hall of Birds as in the human brain. Naturally his colleagues will take this as a critique of neurology. He's grown pessimistic, they'll say, that the study of the brain can explain all of the mental phenomena it is asked to explain. He lets them think that. But actually it is just the opposite. It's not that he's grown pessimistic about the brain, what the brain can explain, it's that he's grown optimistic about birds, what birds can explain . . .

Yes, after her death he comes to realize that his mother was right about birds: it is important to know about them. Each of these taxidermied birds tells us something not only about the natural world but (inasmuch as it was shot by man, brought to the city by man, skinned, stuffed, and sold by man) about the human world as well.

Now, by gazing carefully and continuously at the stuffed white heron that in her waning days gave his mother such peace, he realizes—by means of both his senses and his intuition—that the spirit with which it has been imbued is not a white heron's but rather a young woman's, who was herself most likely reduced to silence by what happened. The neurologist cannot say this definitively, of course, but everything points to it. The neurologist realizes: The naturalist who stuffed this heron must have felt confident that no one would be able to deduce what he'd done, or else he would never have displayed the evidence so publicly! He probably wasn't expecting a museumgoer who by virtue of both personal circumstance and scientific training had such interest and expertise in the growth and atrophy of the linguistic faculty! In language, meaning, ethics, et cetera!

The neurologist writes up his findings and submits them to the world's most prestigious neurological journal, which, however, declines the paper, on the grounds that they cannot understand it, or discern its connection to neurology.

Actually no one can figure out exactly which field the neurologist is working in. The psychopathology journals consider his paper too preoccupied with ethical prescription, the ethics journals consider it too ornithological, the ornithology journals consider it too psychopathological.

In the end, he puts the paper in a drawer. Publication, he realizes, is not the point. The point is not publication but rather the liberation of a spirit from the vessel in which it is trapped.

What he does not realize, my dear Gretel, is that he has fallen in love! Not with the white heron but with the young woman whose exuberant spirit the heron has co-opted! It is as if his mother, who in life was not exactly eager to share her son's affections with another, has led him in death to the woman with whom he'll find happiness!

He doesn't realize it. It is therefore only in *unconscious* expectation of the kind of romantic companionship that until now has always eluded him that the neurologist one Sunday morning shatters the glass of the display case and absconds with the stuffed white heron.

He brings it to that square from which the rubble of the City Theater has only just been hauled away. He places the bird on the cobblestones and starts sawing through the vertebrae of its long kinked neck with a serrated kitchen knife. Only unconsciously is he seeking romantic companionship.

Just then, in the distance, there's an ecstatic cry. He has never made a woman make a sound like that. As he saws through the neck the cry becomes ever more ecstatic until, at the instant he cuts off the heron's head, it joins with the voices of others in a cantata sung with unequaled purity. He runs toward these voices and finally finds himself before the gate of a nunnery. The gate is open. But the Mother Superior, as big as a man, blocks his way. The neurologist tells her: You have among you a nun who is no nun, who, owing to her father's single-minded pursuit of his craft, has been condemned to a perpetual silence of which she has taken no vow, and who in consequence has led the loneliest life imaginable! He informs the Mother Superior that the young woman in question was just then singing in the choir. If only he was allowed to enter . . . But the Mother Superior, glancing doubtfully at the head of the bird he is holding in one hand, and the bird's body he is holding in the other, and also the kitchen knife, permits herself a white lie that she probably feels is justified by the circumstances: But that's a boys' choir! Then she clangs the gate shut and walks quickly away. When she is quite a ways off she laughs derisively and mutters something to herself which the wind carries straight to his ears: Lonely?! It is impossible to express how happy she is, in constant communication with the Lord!

My dear darling Gretel, I miss you so and I kiss you good night!

THE OBSTETRICIAN OBSERVES THE OLD WAYS AGAIN . . .

He is permitted to tag along with the team of illustrious obstetricians attending the Duchess at the birth of her child, but in light of his rank and accent he's instructed not to do or say anything, only to observe.

What he can't help observing, however, is that the swaddled child which the beaming Duchess cradles in her arms, and which she claims emerged from her without the slightest struggle moments before the doctors rushed in, is a doll, a cloth doll with a porcelain head, and (even if she refers to it repeatedly as a boy) a girl doll at that, whose long blond hair has been crudely hacked off. On its ear is a tag from Egerer's Toys.

Yet none of the more senior obstetricians can bring themselves to point that out. When the Duchess asks for their medical opinion of the little boy they all say he looks healthy and strong, not one of them says it's a doll. He has Your Grace's eyes and His Grace's ears, not: It's a doll, look at the tag. They trip over each other to praise the length, weight, and complexion of the child without even mentioning that his head is made of porcelain.

Only the assistant obstetrician remains silent. That does not escape the Duchess, who now demands his opinion. He glances at his superiors. Clears his throat. Even after many years in this city he hasn't learned to be so dexterous with the truth! So what he hears himself saying is that in his judgment it is not a boy at all but a doll, a porcelain doll, and a girl doll at that, whose hair has been hacked off.

All around him he can feel the illustrious obstetricians stiffen. And indeed, the Duchess begins to yell. But not at him. At them. She banishes them from her presence. Everyone out except this young man! And as they close the door behind them they can hear her telling him that at long last she has found an honest doctor.

Now that it is just the two of them, the Duchess begs the assistant obstetrician's forgiveness for the foregoing test. It had to be done to find a doctor she could trust. For while this is indeed a doll, the truth is that she *has* given birth to a baby boy. But the Duke is not the father. The father is the Duke's gamekeeper. If the Duke were to discover that, there is no telling what he would do to the boy, for whom the Duchess has great plans and who is the only creature in the world who can be said to depend completely on her love. That is why the assistant must take him. Please, you must! Just till the boy is big enough to defend himself, then she will come for him . . .

The Duchess calls out the name of a maidservant, who enters with a swaddled infant she carries over to the assistant and places carefully in his arms.

On the one hand, he has never had the least interest in caring for a creature of his own. On the other hand, he reveres the Duchess and is very much moved by her plight. He therefore feels a most ambivalent feeling when, peering down at it, he sees that this, too, is a doll, a cloth doll with a porcelain head. There's an Egerer's tag attached to its ear.

With even greater reluctance than before, the assistant obstetrician is compelled by his conscience and his oath to draw her attention to that fact.

But the Duchess is not upset. She is delighted. Yes! she says. The second test.

The maidservant exits and returns with a third swaddled infant. This time she's remembered to cut off the tag. But still, it's a doll. And it is now clear to the assistant that if there are any more newborns waiting in the wings they, too, will be dolls, all will be dolls, cloth dolls from Egerer's with porcelain heads, whose blond hair has been hacked off.

The Duchess says: My daughters no longer need me, they only need their father, but with this one it's different. Imagine, after seven daddy's girls, a mama's boy! You must take him. You must.

Whether it serves her interests, psychiatrically, to pass any more of her "tests" seems doubtful to him. So he accepts the doll and takes it home. In doing so he has not strayed from the truth because he never explicitly conceded that it was a living creature. Nevertheless, he is troubled. His medical training cannot tell him whether in accepting the Duchess's doll he did the right thing. He therefore buries the doll deep in his closet and does his utmost to forget the whole incident.

Yet the medical establishment, humiliated before their own Duchess by a Slavic upstart from their empire's most backward province, has no intention of letting him forget it. First they try to cajole him into divulging what happened after their expulsion. When they fail to extract that from him they begin to persecute him. They stalk him through the ward. No longer can he examine patients or perform procedures without a superior watching his every move. The orderlies harass him with their mops, the nurses countermand his orders. Formerly close colleagues make him repeat himself again and again as if they cannot possibly comprehend him through an accent which, in point of fact, is so faint as to be basically nonexistent. They innocently inquire about the ethnic significance of his hat—a hat they know perfectly well was purchased right here, in the city, and at one of the most high-end hatters! They inquire about the ethnic significance of his trousers. Trousers that were purchased here. All of this is to impress on the assistant that he isn't one of them and never will be, no matter how much he dresses like them, no matter how deeply he succeeds in drilling their tongue into his brain. That his pathological adherence to the truth is a primitive relic of a people and a place he has not transcended, and never will, not even if he lives in the city for a thousand years.

At last he is obliged to quit the clinic and go into private practice. Even still, the torment continues. No sooner has he begun building his practice than an appalling rumor finds its way to his patients. That he had confined a child to a closet in his home. That this child lived its brief life in absolute darkness. That it never knew to wail since it had no awareness of the existence of others. That because he had deprived this child of all possible concepts, including space and time and cause and effect, its psyche could not even be imaginatively entered into by those sympathetic souls who yearned to have a sense of how it suffered before it died. And that such things are commonplace among the South Slavs.

How easy it would be to put this rumor to rest! He'd need only show the world the doll, the world would see it wasn't a child.

And if the medical establishment circled the wagons and tried to pretend it was a child, that claim could easily be proved false. But not without betraying the confidence of the Duchess. Not without exposing her to ridicule. And that is something the obstetrician won't do. For even as he loses his illusions about the city he preserves his reverence for the family at its heart.

This reverence comes at a terrible cost. He loses his patients and his practice. In upholding the dignity of the Duchess, he falls into destitution.

In order to survive the obstetrician pawns all of his belongings. First his fashionable hat and trousers, then everything else. Finally the only thing remaining in his closet is the traditional festive costume of his homeland and the porcelain doll that caused all of his woes. He hasn't laid eyes on either of them in years. Neither is exactly as he remembers it. The doll is a little smaller, the festive costume a little more elegant. When he came to the city he brought the festive costume with him only to placate his mother, whose heart would have been broken had he left it behind. She insisted he would find occasion to wear it. How he had laughed at that! But now he sees that his mother was right. He puts on the traditional festive costume. And not only because he has nothing else. He is wearing it because he wants to.

He holds the doll to his breast and sings it the Slavic folk songs that were sung to him as a child.

After a few such episodes he begins to feel, strange to say, that he is transforming into a mother himself, with the stupendous self-sufficiency of a mother. The borders of his world shrink vertiginously. He begins to feel that the empire can do with him what it will so long as it leaves him this creature to care for.

Of course he knows that he is not a mother, that he can never be a mother, not really. An obstetrician stands close to motherhood but always apart from it. He can't *become* a mother. Yet he feels exactly like one. He could even swear that something is growing inside of him. He does not know what it is. But he can feel it moving.

One day he receives a coded communiqué from the office of the Duchess. The communiqué states, in effect, that the Duchess's doll is to be returned to her. That is all. There is no mention of restitution. There is not even an expression of gratitude.

The porcelain doll is as much his now as it is hers. He, too, has great plans for it. However, he knows he has no choice but to return it to her. And he intends to do so, just as soon as he knits it a festive costume of its own.

He knits it the costume.

Then, in the stuffing of the doll, by means of an incision concealed by this festive costume, he implants an incendiary device set to go off at a date and time of his choosing.

Then he sends the doll to the ducal residence.

Yes, something really is growing inside of him! The obstetrician can feel it kicking and thrashing. It's impatient, it is ready to be born, it yearns to see the light of day. But it's not a fetus. No, it is no fetus. It's a nation-state.

P

THE PUPIL COMPOSES POETRY EVEN WHILE POSING FOR THE PAINTER . . .

She weeps on a park bench beside a fountain that has completely frozen over and across from which, unbeknownst to her, she is being carefully observed by a painter with the soul of a youngster.

This painter, for whom it was a tragedy that he should have grown so big and tall inasmuch as he looms far above the very people to whom he feels closest, now circles round the fountain and sits down beside her.

Why is she sad?

But the pupil shakes her head.

She is not supposed to speak to strangers.

Only gradually does he get it out of her. How she had written a poem . . . How the poem was intended to please her father . . . But how he hadn't even listened to it to the end . . .

My dear child! the painter cries. (His heart is bursting.) My dear child, grown-ups in this city don't know the first thing about art!

He himself was once enrolled at the city's most prestigious academy of art, but he'd been asked to leave because no one considered his renderings of children to be realistic. Children, he was told, aren't like that. Now, setting aside the question of whether art should even aim to reproduce reality, the fact of the matter is: Children *are* like that! They are! That is *precisely* what children are like! Children are capable of extraordinary things, of good as well as evil. The burghers deny it but their own children know it. Is it any wonder that he should have come to prefer the company of the young? In truth it was a blessing to leave the Academy of Fine Arts, since he no longer had to pretend that he had anything in common with those of his age, or that he was moved by their art. The great secret about the art of grown-ups (this is whispered into the pupil's ear) is that it is all too *arty*. It is too late for them to be naive and so all their art succumbs to artiness . . .

My child, the painter says, I should very much like to hear your poem. And in return I shall paint a picture of you.

He offers her his hand, she takes it, and they proceed like that to the painter's studio.

On her fifth day there her father, a dealer on the stock exchange, finally tracks her down. Now, the father has always regarded the daughter as an extension of himself rather than an autonomous being with an inner life of her own. In this he is absolutely paradigmatic of his class. He therefore barges into the painter's studio armed with all sorts of misapprehensions. In order to placate him, the painter offers to sell him the portrait he has just completed at a price significantly lower than what it would fetch at a gallery. But from the father's response to this offer the painter is able to deduce something inexpressibly sad: that he doesn't even know what his own daughter looks like. When he looks at this painting he does not know what he is seeing. And it is not just the angle and outfit that are foreign to him, it's the very idea of her as someone separate from himself.

The father addresses her: Get your things, we're going.

In response to which the pupil indicates that she is going nowhere.

Naturally the burgher finds it impossible to imagine that she might indicate that of her own volition. His failure of imagination can't help but elicit the painter's sympathy since it is less he than his class that doesn't attribute a will to its young. But when he moves to seize his daughter, the painter, who looms above not only the pupil but also her father, steps forward to intervene.

There is nothing wrong with hosting young people in his studio. Nothing. Yet from the instant the burgher departs the painter knows that it will no longer be possible to remain in the city proper. God forbid the children of the bourgeoisie, accustomed to seeing the doors to their fathers' offices swing shut in their faces, should have a place to go where a working artist acknowledges the richness of their psyches and familiarizes them with the methodologies of his art! That is not how the city will choose to see it, however. He knows that. The bourgeois order will see in him a threat to itself. That even a single grown-up should treat children as equals who know about good and evil and can choose their own ends: this threatens to undermine the lie on which the city stands.

The painter and the pupil take a tram to the end of the line, proceed into the woods, and stumble upon an abandoned mill. At first the mill frightens the pupil. But beneath the peeling white-wash there are signs of a fresco depicting hundreds and hundreds of merry little children, and that is presented to her as an auspicious sign.

Indeed, their life there is an idyll.

In the mornings they take a stroll in the woods. Then the pupil writes poetry and the painter paints her. Her simple little poems with their strange leaps of logic strike the painter as possessing something like genius, and his paintings of her, dispatched to a dealer in the city, fetch prices that support them both. He restores the fresco and, in a parody of bourgeois domesticity, hangs flowerboxes beneath the windows.

In short, seclusion suits them.

Yet it turns out that they are less secluded than they think. One day they hear someone blow a horn in the woods and when they look out the window they see no fewer than thirty children sprinting toward them, followed by their elderly teacher. The pupil starts to wave and whoop, but the painter suggests that they maintain absolute silence and flatten themselves against the walls.

So, the painter thinks: There must be an elementary school nearby.

After that they guard their solitude even more vigilantly.

Still, they stroll, they paint, they compose.

Alas, nothing lasts . . .

It is the peculiar burden of the eternal child to be perpetually outgrown by one's playmates. For the young at heart the world is always wilting; one sees one's friends die before their time. It pains the painter to admit this but the pupil's thoughts, which once gamboled about in the most mischievous fashion, come by degrees under the yoke of a sober bourgeois logic. Simply put, she is growing up. As he loses access to her inner world, his paintings suffer accordingly, and this is reflected in the prices they fetch.

Perhaps she can sense what is happening, for she starts to strike new and unusual poses. But that, of course, is not the issue. If the painter could grow up with her, he would, but he can't! He can't. In this respect his massive size and height have always been misleading.

He wanders into the woods and there weeps and wails as loud as if he had just buried the pupil deep in the ground. He returns to the mill by way of the nearby school, accompanied by a schoolgirl with artistic inclinations.

First he paints the pupil and the schoolgirl together. Then, and thereafter, he paints the schoolgirl alone.

At night the pupil recites long poems that have become as calculated and sentimental as any crowd-pleasing play. They strive for effect and the effect they are striving for is obvious. They even attempt moral instruction. Although the painter tries to stay awake until she has finished he does not always succeed in this.

One morning he informs the pupil that he has had a dream which in its clarity comes close to a vision. In this dream she returned to her father's house, and he, rather than slamming the door shut in her face, wordlessly welcomed her in.

He leaves a tram token on the table and then strolls alone in the woods. But when he returns to the mill it is the schoolgirl, not the pupil, who is gone. The pupil holds in her hands a round object wrapped in a bedsheet. She recounts what happened:

The schoolgirl's mother had come, a typical bourgeois. Quick, quick, the mother said, get your things, let's go! This you can leave here, however. This you won't need.

Now he knows what is wrapped in the sheet. It's the schoolgirl's head. He takes the tram into the city to tell the authorities what the pupil has done. But of course they do not believe him. How does he know it wasn't a ball she was holding, or a balloon? They simply cannot imagine a child doing anything but play. Indeed, they seem more interested in his activities than in hers, for it is only grown-ups (they imagine) who perform acts of moral consequence. The irony is that he, as an artist, really *is* engaged in "play," whereas she has become too mature for that! None of this makes any impression on the authorities. And a subsequent inquiry to the elementary school brings to light the happy news that the schoolgirl turned up alive and well. That gives a big boost to the theory that what was wrapped in the sheet was a ball or balloon. So be it, let it be a ball. In this particular instance the pupil was playing. That doesn't alter the fact that she, like every child, is as capable as any grown-up of doing great good and tremendous evil. And if you do not credit children with evil, you cannot credit them with goodness either . . .

His insistence on this last point was what eventually landed the painter in the Sanatorium Dr. Krakauer. The pupil, meanwhile, is all grown up now and doing very well. She has dined out for years on this interesting episode from her youth; that sort of thing goes quite far in the theater world. Not to take anything away from her accomplishments! Only, it is all so *arty* now. She sets her little librettos in places she knows only from books, this one in Montenegro, that one in—

Andalusia, I suggest.

Yes, yes, Andalusia, the painter murmurs. He is one of those lunatics too little invested in the existence of others to be surprised by what they know. Andalusia, that's right. I can't imagine it is any good.

Q

THE QUARRYMAN QUESTIONS ALL THIS ABOUT THE STRING QUARTET . . .

Construction commences on the New City Theater. But quickly it comes to a halt. And why so, my dear Gretel? Well, the distinguished professor of architecture who'd won the right to build it complains that the stone has come from the quarry in an unusable condition, every slab scratched and scarred. It is maintained at first by Holzinger, the quarry owner, that the markings in question are simply the natural striations of the stone, but he concedes in the end that they must have been made by human hands. He turns up a culprit, a quarryman who, inasmuch as the professor's design for the new theater is completely inimical to the art of drama, becomes an object of reverence at the Sanatorium Dr. Krakauer even before an unknown benefactor puts him up here. But the quarryman insists that he does not know what everyone is talking about. He is a simple man, he says: he knows nothing about arts and culture. A simple man, simple, no arts, no culture. He claims to know nothing about the neo-Baroque, and everyone begins to believe him. He slashes at the air first with one hand—No arts!—then with the other—No culture!—and then gives the following account of what happened at the quarry:

He had two children, Oskar and Ottilie.

Ottilie was the complicated one, Oskar the simple one.

She told lies, he told the truth.

But he loved them the same, exactly the same.

For that is one's duty as a father: to love the complicated lying child just as much as the simple truth-teller.

One day they came to him with the question of why they had no mother, as all the other children did. And he, to spare them the guilt of knowing that theirs had died giving them life, made the mistake of telling them that she had gone to live deep underground in a palace in the earth and was living there still in a state of perfect contentment.

After that he could not keep Ottilie out of the tunnels of the quarry. He warned her of the dangers, but she wouldn't listen. And wherever Ottilie went Oskar went also.

Eventually what he feared would happen did happen: they went into the tunnels and did not come back out. Search parties returned empty-handed. At night Lucifer came to him where he lay in his bed and offered to give back one of the two children if he would simply say the name of the child he wanted back more. *Don't* say you love them the same. He woke up bathed in sweat. But the village priest assured him that these visions were merely the product of his own anguished mind.

In the end Ottilie emerged from the mouth of the tunnel and Oskar did not. She came out hale and hearty, and when she leapt into his arms—*Papa!*—he was surprised by how heavy she was. When, however, he asked her how that could be, and what had happened to Oskar, she burst into tears and said she did not want to talk about it, she just wanted to go home.

He took her home, but there the tears ceased and she began to whistle.

So he seized her by the shoulders and demanded again to know what had happened.

He knew, of course, that she would lie, for she had always been a liar, but the lie she told this time was so fanciful that it was as if she no longer cared to be believed by him:

I know you're lying when you tell us our mother is still alive, but Oskar believes you. He always begged me to go into the tunnels with him. I'm his sister, so I always went. This time we went deeper than we'd ever gone before. Then our torch went out so we turned around to go back. But after a while we realized we had not been going up after all, we'd still been going down! Then we knew we were lost. And we were hungry and thirsty so we thought we were going to die! But then I heard music coming from down below. At first Oskar couldn't hear it, but as we got closer he could. Then we came into a cavern where a string quartet was playing. They had all sorts of snacks, and we were allowed to have the snacks, no one from the string quartet stopped us! We ate and drank whatever we wanted and listened to the quartet play. I probably could've listened forever because I loved it and I thought the music was *marvelous* but Oskar put his hands over his ears because he thought it was too modern. When they were done we clapped and told them we were lost and asked if they knew how we could get back home. And the quartet said that yes, they knew. And they told us this tale: Once there was a quarryman who fell in love with a maiden. He wished to marry her but first he needed to get rid of the wife he had already because as long as she was around the priest refused to conduct the ceremony. So he carried his wife deep into the tunnels of the quarry. The wife was surprised because she still enjoyed her husband's company and was quite content with married life, but obviously he felt differently since here he was hauling her into the earth. She kicked and thrashed and scratched at the walls, but he was strong and nothing could hinder his progress. In the pitch-black bowels of the quarry he left her to die. Yet so attached was she to their life as she knew it that in stone which usually yields only to the blow of a chisel, her fingernails had left long, deep lines. That accounts for the wonderful striations of this world-famous stone. And by feeling her way along the lines she had made she found her way to the surface and back to her husband's house. But her time underground must have enfeebled her mind, for when she set eyes on the girl who now lay in her bed she spoke to her as if the girl were her daughter. And if this was her daughter, then the quarryman must be her son-in-law. That suited everyone, she lived there like their mother, mending their clothing and begging them please to bless her with a grandchild. The end. Then the quartet showed us the lines in the wall and said that if we followed them we'd find our way out. But Oskar saw that the lines also went the other way, deeper underground. He whispered: This must be the antechamber of the palace, Mother must be nearby! Nothing could convince him she was dead, because why would Father lie? We had no choice but to split up. I turned back and Oskar went on. As soon as I was alone in the tunnel I had to wonder, Did any of that truly happen? But then I heard the music start up behind me, so I knew that it truly had.

As soon as she finished Ottilie started to whistle again. Her father knew that by telling him such claptrap she was daring him to call her a liar. But he would not give her that satisfaction. Instead he told her that he loved her and was overjoyed to have her back.

Lucifer visited him in his dreams. The girl is a complicated person! No one could fault you for preferring the company of the boy. It is not too late: Hand her over to me and I will return him to you. And Lucifer proceeded to outline the highly specific scenario in which the exchange might be effected. The quarryman declined because he loved them the same.

This went on night after night until at last he sought relief from the priest. He explained that his visions could not possibly be the product of his own mind because the scenario Lucifer proposed relied on a kind of knowledge the quarryman did not possess. Knowledge, namely, of arts and culture. The priest sprinkled him with holy water and banished Lucifer from his presence.

That night the Devil did not visit him. Nor did he come again in all the nights that followed. It was therefore reasonable to suppose that his offer had been revoked.

Years went by. The quarryman grew older, and so did his daughter. She was roundly regarded as mad because she spent all of her time wandering and whistling in the hills around the quarry and would not recant her story of what had happened deep within it.

Then, one day, a new laborer came to work in the quarry. Everyone could see that there was something strange about him. He wore the same work clothes as everyone else, the same work cap. But he failed to conceal the fanciness of his shoes. And while he tried to restrict himself to the coarse idioms of his fellow quarrymen, it soon became impossible to ignore the immensity of his vocabulary.

Now, in the city such nice shoes and big words would pass without notice, because such things are plentiful there. But the Holzinger Quarry is a far cry from the city!

Rumors circulated . . . It was said, for example, that the man was a highborn aristocrat. That he was a Holzinger himself. That his family was as wealthy as they come. That the city's artistic institutions owed their existence to the family's munificence. That he possessed the largest private collection of military paraphernalia in continental Europe. But that that had not satisfied him, he also wanted to write a brief study on "The history of the idea of the atom from Democritus to Mayrhofer." That he'd written half the study, got stuck, and in consequence wanted to die. That in order to go on living, he needed to cease thinking. But that so long as he remained within the city limits that was impossible, since the city is such a thought-provoking place. That his doctor ordered him to commit himself to a simple trade that would exhaust his body among simple people in a simple place where thoughts never develop to the point where they need forcibly to be extinguished. And that that was how he came to be there . . .

At first no one trusted him, everyone resented him. But in time he endeared himself to them, all the more so when he put down his hammer and chisel, with which he was worthless, and dedicated himself to the edification of their young. He lined the empty shelves of their schoolhouse with mathematical textbooks and taught them the names of the constellations. He took the children into the city to see the stuffed birds at the Natural History

Museum and the pickled brains at the Pathological-Anatomical Institute. He even tried to include Ottilie. He chased after her as she went whistling in the hills and tried to persuade her father that she had the capacity to learn. Her lies he called acting, her whistling he called music! She appeared mad here only because this was not her proper habitat. If the quarryman would just let him take her to the City Theater . . .

One evening the man arranged at the quarry a performance by a string quartet which, less because they liked or understood the music than because they felt included at last in the cultural life of the city, brought tears to the eyes of the wives of the quarrymen.

But the final piece the quartet played was liked and understood by everyone, because everyone, to their own astonishment, recognized it: it was the tune Ottilie was always whistling.

Naturally, this was nothing but a magic trick orchestrated by the rich man, who must have commissioned the piece. The quarryman realized that. But no one else did. Instead they gave credence to her lies and regarded her as an artist whose talents had been kept from developing by a father who had never understood her. Everything complicated about her was suddenly seen instead as something artistic about her. If he cared for his daughter in the least he would let the man take her to the City Theater!

He tried to convince everyone that this was clearly a dangerous individual who shouldn't be entrusted with their children. He pointed out how strange it was that a rich man who obviously held them in contempt should set about trying to rescue as many of their children as he could from the very life his own doctor had prescribed for him. But the other quarrymen had already been won over by the donation of the textbooks, and the compliance of their wives had been obtained with the quartet. The women were willing to disregard the fact that their children were in danger because they had gotten the gift of an evening of music. Better to call Ottilie's father mad, better to call him a liar.

All this took a toll on him. One can hold on to the truth for only so long when the whole world claims one is in possession of a falsehood. Perhaps Ottilie *was* an artist, perhaps he didn't have the ears to hear it. He vowed from now on to keep her happiness in view. So when the man came to him a third time and asked to take Ottilie to the City Theater—a play was premiering, *The Lieutenant's Daughter*—and she whispered, *Please, Papa!*, he did not say no, but rather squeezed her shoulder and gave his blessing. Only after they left did he realize that the terms of art and culture the man used sounded familiar. They were the exact words used by Lucifer. So he knew what would happen next. That the theater would go up in flames, that the rich man, who knew all of its ins and outs, and was, moreover, an emissary of the Devil, would escape unscathed, but that Ottilie would perish. Yet it cannot be said that the quarryman agreed to this, since one cannot agree to what one can't understand.

No, he knows nothing about arts and culture! Still, a deal is a deal. So the instant he heard what had happened to Ottilie he ran into the tunnels to greet Oskar. At first he thought that the Devil had tricked him because the boy did not emerge from the depths of hell. But when he reached out a hand to steady himself against the stone he realized that he was able now to decipher its striations, of which Oskar was obviously the author. Thus the boy really was returned to him, if not in the form he expected. And what his son was writing made him laugh, because it was simple and true. As the quarryman read the walls with both hands he could not quiet a voice which pointed out that the girl, for all her virtues, had never made him laugh like this. Then he took up his tools and responded in kind.

And that, he concludes, is what happened at the quarry.

Now, the distinguished professor behind the New City Theater is a devout Catholic. He quits the project as soon as this story comes to light. And after that no one will touch it. Everyone calls it cursed.

The sole exception is the architect you'll recall who, in building a building for a high-end jeweler, happened to incur the displeasure of the ducal family.

The Duke and Duchess object strenuously to his involvement; Dr. Krakauer recommends that he remain locked up. Yet so ravenous is the hunger of the city for drama that the municipal authorities are compelled in the end to order his release.

In a newspaper interview the architect explains his intentions:

Every theater from antiquity to the present has been built in ignorance of the anatomy of the child! Even when the child cranes her neck to the utmost she still can't see a thing, because her seat is too low and the heads of the grown-ups too high! For the child everything is dark and muffled, it is less a theater than a womb! It is not the child's fault that she is always nodding off at the theater, all warm and cozy and alienated from the spectacle! Nor is it that children lack the capacity to understand what is happening onstage! His theater will be simple, simpler even than that of the Greeks, and it will permit the children to see as well as the grown-ups do! In fact there is only one seat in the whole house from which the view can be said to be *completely* unobstructed, and it is a seat upon which a child will sit.

R

THE REVOLUTIONARY REVEALS HERSELF TO BE A REVI-
SIONIST IN HER OWN RIGHT . . .

For its reluctance to call a general strike, the Russian revolutionary in exile accuses her adopted city's party executive of
revisionism.

The executive, for its part, prefers to win piecemeal victories by
parliamentary means because it knows that the present somno-
lence of the city's working class would doom such a strike from
the outset.

The executive is also well aware that if not for this woman's spell
in a tsarist prison and the aura of martyrdom that resulted from
it, which she has nurtured with the skill of a master propagandist,
no one would take seriously her claim to know what the masses
of a foreign city are thinking.

At last the revolutionary proposes settling their differences by setting aside their speculations about the mental state of the masses
and instead consulting the masses directly.

To that end she brings to the coffeehouse an actual member of the
masses.

And not just any member of the masses but a man who, for reasons she will explain, can even be considered the quintessence of

the masses. She introduces to the party executive the middle-aged man she's pushing in a wheelchair, who, she points out, has lost all four of his limbs and for that reason answers to the name the Rump Man, or the Human Torso.

Lost, she adds, to an industrial machine . . .

But look! And she puts before him a glass of water which, by pressing it against his head with the stump of one arm, the man is able to lift up and drink down.

And now listen, she says. Even though she had no friends in this city, and no family save an estranged aunt, and even though she had alienated powerful members of the party by telling the truth about their revisionist efforts to wring concessions for the masses from the existing order, she felt when she arrived here that she would not be lonely inasmuch as she had always considered herself to be at one with the working class everywhere. When not hauling home books from the Municipal Library or scribbling away in her spartan room, she was out walking the streets among the masses. Yet something about the way she walked set her apart from the masses. Even when she picked out a face coming toward her down the street, and smiled at it, as often as not it did not smile back. Was there, and this of course ran counter to every internationalist bone in her body, something ineradicably Russian about her? Her posture? Her step? Why did the masses resist her? But as she watched them strolling in their rose gardens and enjoying their rich confections, it suddenly dawned on her: these weren't the masses at all, these were the middle and upper-middle classes! The masses were elsewhere. She searched for them. At last she found them, at the edge of the city, in an amusement park beloved by their class. There she was swallowed up by the masses and borne by them deeper and deeper into the park, past pleasures that grew more marvelously vulgar with every step. She ate greasy meat skewered on a stick, guzzled down big mugs of beer, surrendered herself body and soul to the earthy rhythms of the hurdy-gurdy man. With every step she could sense that she was coming closer and closer to the heart of the people. In the center of the park she parted the flaps of a tent and entered the freak show. First a man came out who was much too big, then a woman who was much too small. The masses clapped. The third act withstood a blow in the chest with a mallet, the masses hooted, they liked that very much. The fourth had too much hair everywhere, the masses roared, they loved that! Yet all this was only a prelude to the fifth and final act, who, as the revolutionary realized the moment he was wheeled onstage in a little wooden wagon, was of extraordinary significance to the class struggle . . .

The Russian revolutionary now turns to the Rump Man: Sir, please tell these gentlemen how you lost your limbs.

So, the man says, I was working in this factory that made these little . . . thingies, 'bout yea big, I dunno what you call 'em, no one told us what they were for but we had to churn out a whole helluva lot of 'em. So one day I'm working the machine, the main machine, the real big one, and what does it do but grab my arm and yank that sucker like a bitch! Yow! So I'm yellin' and hollerin' and carryin' on, tryin' to pull my arm out and whatnot, but the machine's too effing strong, so what I do is, I get one of my legs round and push against the machine to get some, whaddya call it, *leverage* on it, right? But what happens is, instead of getting my arm *out* of it, my leg goes *into* it, right, and now *that* sucker starts getting yanked like a bitch! Then Herr K. comes out on the balcony, he's the owner, he's got his fingers in his ears on account of the ruckus and he says it's no use pulling or pushing, I gotta hit the effing off switch on the back. So I'm reaching round with my free arm, I'm feeling for the off switch, feeling for the off switch, feeling for the off switch, when, kapow! Yanked like a bitch! Yow! Right? So now I only got the one leg free and I'm thinking: Well, shucks! Who the hell's gonna hire a one-legged man? In this day and age? And no arms, neither? And it's even worse than that, cuz when I come to, even that last leg's gone, right? Guess they had to cut it off also. It seemed fine to me, but what do I know?

Gentlemen, says the Russian revolutionary, spreading her arms with satisfaction: Surely you can see why I now like to say that "the road to the Revolution runs right through the Rump Man." Here is the proletariat of the proletariat, in whom the working class beholds its fate if it does not rise up and withhold its labor. And so I ask you, she says, turning back to him: Do you support a general strike?

Oh, yes, the man says. Yessiree.

Yessiree, she says. And with a sly smile she excuses herself so that the executive might ponder this.

But it is something quite different that the party executive is pondering, namely who this man really is. For no native speaker would be fooled for a moment by his imitation of a working-class accent. And the man must know that, too, because as soon as he sees the Russian revolutionary go into the restroom he whispers:

Please, I shall tell you the truth, but I beg of you not to tell her! I have, needless to say, never set foot in a factory. First I was the *maître de ballet* and subsequently the General Intendant of the old City Theater, in whose dreadful conflagration I lost the younger of my daughters, as well as my limbs. In my art I had always prized simplicity and naturalness of gesture. That I now had to teach myself de novo how to drink a glass of water and bring a forkful of food to my mouth, how to wash and dress and relieve myself, therefore struck me as a grotesque parody of my artistic ambitions. I knew God had done this to me. I betook myself to the freak show, He brought me there. And every time I came out onstage before the leering masses I thought, Yes, I am a "freak," but not for the reasons you think! I am a freak because in my effort to isolate the fundamental "atom" of human movement, I have trespassed on a realm of naturalness and simplicity from which the good Lord had banished us. In short, I smuggled my wife and daughters back into the Garden, and when He found us there he struck down two of them, sent the last to Russia, and tore off my arms and legs to boot. There is simple, and there is over-simple; simple is good, oversimple less so. In a roundabout way, this brought me back to classical ballet, with which I'd begun my career but which only now was I in a position to understand. True, it was neither simple nor natural. But that was the virtue of it. To my daughter in St. Petersburg I wrote letters care of the Imperial Ballet. I wanted to apologize for certain things I'd once said about the classical vocabulary. But the letters came back to me unopened—and fair enough, as I'd done the same to the letters she'd sent me as a student. And so I expected nothing more from life. Alone amongst the terrible masses I would do my penance and then die. Yet one evening, when I came onstage, there, in the audience, was my daughter. Her face was lined now, her hair white, and she tried to conceal her balletic grace by rounding her shoulders like one of the downtrodden. But I knew it was she. And when she came backstage and spoke to me in a Russian accent, that confirmed it. But though I knew it was she, I realized that she did not know it was I. She kept referring to me as "a member of the masses," or "the proletariat of the proletariat." If she found out who I really was I knew she'd leave without another word, so I spent the whole night spinning tales about life on the factory floor. Again and again she wanted to hear the story of what capitalism had done to my limbs. About the callous factory owner who'd plugged his ears to block my screams, and so forth. If I have any value to her it is only as an allegorical tableau of the exploitation of man by man, I know that, but that's all right, I'm just happy to be near her! My artistic ambitions are dead and gone, I just want to spend time with my daughter. So I tell her whatever I have to tell her: Yes, I want a general strike, yes, the other freaks want a general strike, everyone wants a general strike, a general strike would be a tremendous success, et cetera. All nonsense, of course: the freaks are perfectly content with the status quo and a general strike would collapse before it began. Okay, here she comes! *Please don't tell her!* So fellas, that's why we gotta smash the effing Serbs, yow! Kapow! Oh, hallo again.

Now, the executive already knew the revolutionary to be deluded about the mood of the masses. But if it is true the Rump Man is her father, then her delusions run even deeper than that. Certainly they could win a quick victory by revealing this. Yet to expose her delusions would risk ridding her of them. And the executive regard her as less of a threat to them deluded than not. Because whatever claim the revolutionary might have had to the mantle of Marx was lost the moment she installed at the heart of her system of supposedly "scientific" socialism the Romantic figure of the Rump Man. *The road to the Revolution runs through the Rump Man*: This can hardly be called orthodox Marxism. If it is un-Marxist to put one's faith in the parliamentary process, how much more so to put it in the Rump Man! Yes, the more her analysis of history relies on the concept of the Rump Man, the less imperiled they are by her accusations of revisionism. And it occurs to them that nothing would put a stop to the fantasy of a general strike like letting her call one in which only two people participate, a father and a daughter, neither from the working class, both rather from the world of ballet . . .

It is resolved: There will be a "general strike." The revolutionary and the Rump Man will lead it.

As the revolutionary wheels the Rump Man away she can't help but exult at the outcome of the meeting. The Rump Man, too, can't help but exult. The party executive can't help but exult. Even the coffeehouse lunatic, who won a dozen new souls for his expedition to the north, can't help but exult. Everyone is in agreement: it could not have gone better. And what a rarity that is among socialist congresses of the Second International!

Good night!

S

THE SATIRIST SPEAKS . . .

Never before has the sweet, simple man gone to see him speak, because until now he has always been afraid that he would not understand what the satirist had to say.

He was afraid he would laugh at the wrong moment.

Or fail to laugh at a moment that called for laughter.

And that in doing so he would embarrass his mother.

It therefore made him glad when she left him alone in the apartment to go see the satirist, because then she could enjoy the satirist's wit without worrying about her son's incomprehension.

These speeches by the satirist, whom she calls the cleverest man in the city, are the only occasions on which his mother allows herself the luxury of leaving him alone. Otherwise she has to care for him around the clock. She feeds him and cleans him and attends to his intimate necessities. He knows enough to know what his mother has given up for him, and even if he does not have the words to express what this means to him, he has his own ways of showing his affection. He nuzzles her with his nose, or touches her hair with the tips of his fingers.

He is the cleverest, she tells him, meaning the satirist: But you are the sweetest.

He knows enough to know how hard it must be for such a sophisticated woman to spend every waking hour with someone like him, who has such trouble understanding things. Once upon a time she made sculptures out of stone, she knew all of the stars in the sky, she read long books about how society works. And then he came along, and everything changed. His father left because no one wants to be saddled with a son who has no understanding. But she, of course, did not leave. She took him from speech clinician to speech clinician, from neurologist to neurologist. Not one of them could diagnose him; and because they were unable to put a name to what was wrong with him, they wrote down in their files that nothing was wrong. That is how doctors are. But she knew early on that he would never be able to live on his own, never make a friend or fall in love, never feed himself, or clean himself, or attend to his own intimate necessities. He would never stop needing her. And that meant no more sculptures, no more stars, no more books about society. Yet never for a second did she think of giving him away, not even when the state got the idea that it could turn him into a soldier.

He must not feel guilty, though. You are my sweet, simple boy!

Of course, he does feel guilty. If not for him she would have been a world-famous sculptor or stargazer, she would have had world-famous thoughts about how society works. Instead for forty years she has done nothing but take care of him. That is why it makes him happy when she goes to hear the satirist speak. There she finds herself among her own people. People who understand everything, instead of nothing. One searches in vain for a single stupid face. She spends all day beforehand getting ready and half the night afterward telling him about it: the luminaries in attendance, the gales of knowledgeable laughter, the endless ovations. Everything except what the satirist actually said, which, inasmuch as he would not understand it, would only cause him pain.

Only once does he ask: What if he tried really hard to understand? What if he tried really, really, *really* hard to understand?

Even still, she says, kissing his brow and smiling in such a sad way that he never dares ask that question again: Even still, you would not.

Then the next performance rolls around. On such days they always wake up early out of sheer excitement. She tries on all of her dresses and jewelry and he gets to do all of her buttons and clasps. But this morning she does not wake up early. She does not even wake up by noon. His mother is very old now, her skin hangs down from her bones, and he knows enough to know that very old people need a great deal of sleep. She does not even wake up by four. He thinks: I shall let her sleep until one hour before it begins, and then I shall have to rouse her.

He has never been alone this long.

Thrown back on his own resources, the sweet, simple man makes a surprising discovery. He discovers that he is able to feed and clean himself and even attend to his intimate necessities.

And if he can do all that, what else can he do?

It occurs to him to wonder if he might actually understand what the satirist has to say.

So that evening, rather than rousing his mother, he takes her ticket and goes off to see the satirist himself.

The satirist has already begun speaking when the sweet, simple man arrives. He takes his seat and tries his best to understand:

. . . the poor Chief of the General Staff! They call him single-minded but that's only because they don't understand the seriousness of the Serbian threat. That's why in the newspaper one always finds him seriously studying the map of the Balkans. No one understands, not even his wife, let alone the sovereign. Twenty-two times he's proposed preemptive war with Serbia, and twenty-two times the sovereign has said no. And Russia's becoming a colossus, soon it'll be too late. Suddenly the Chief of the General Staff sits up straight at his desk, where he's been studying his map of the Balkans. Wait a second— What if—? Actually, it's an interesting idea! He grabs his hat. What if he proposes it a twenty-third time?! But the sovereign says no. He's on the floor playing dolls with his daughter, he doesn't even bother to look up. He exclaims: *My policy is a policy of peace!* For reasons that baffle the Chief of the General Staff the sovereign does not take Serbia seriously. He returns to the Ministry, returns to the map of the Balkans, and studies it with the utmost seriousness, the resulting photographs all reflect that. Then his wife demands a weekend in the Alps. Now?! She does not take Serbia seriously and never has. They follow a ski instructor into the mountains of St. Wolfgang. The air grows thin; they stop at the top to catch their breath; the Chief of the General Staff takes the opportunity to immerse himself in his map of the Balkans; and something snaps in the missus. When was the last time he looked at her the way he looks at the Kingdom of Serbia? She helps the strapping young ski instructor off with his rucksack and urges him to ravish her right there in the snow. Don't worry, my husband's *completely* immersed in the Balkans. Later on, back at the Ministry, the Chief of the General Staff examines the photographs from their weekend away to see which has the greatest propaganda value vis-à-vis the Serbs. Here he is in a lodge, studying the map of the Balkans. Here he is beside a tree, studying the map of the Balkans. And here he is on a mountaintop, studying the map of the Balkans. This last one's perfect: the snow, the sky, the seriousness of his expression as he studies the map of the Balkans. When Pašić sees that one plastered in the papers he'll know that the Chief of the General Staff has his number! But wait a second— What's this—? He squints at the photo. And what he sees in the background throws him into a deep depression. Because the way that his wife is getting ravished by the ski instructor will no doubt diminish the propaganda value of the photograph. It hardly matters how seriously he's studying the Balkans if his wife is getting ravished in the background by a fine-looking young man in a feathered Tyrolean hat. He's not naive when it comes to the press, he knows the ravishing of his wife cuts the photo's propaganda value at least in half. Because a piece of propaganda, if it is to be effective, must be simple and unequivocal, understandable at a glance, but the messaging of this photograph is ambiguous: In the foreground strength and sangfroid, in the background something else. They'll have to go with the one in the lodge. But sir! (It's Scolik, the court photographer.) Sir, that's easily fixed! And with a pair of scissors Scolik simply cuts away everything in the photograph that doesn't directly impinge on the Serbian threat. The Chief of the General Staff is delighted; today he feels he has done his part to save the monarchy. The photo appears in the *Neue Freie Presse*. The problem is, in snipping off the coition Scolik accidentally cut off a corner of the map showing a portion of Serbia claimed by Bulgaria. And that has serious international repercussions. Sazonov knocks over his samovar, Poincaré spits out his croissant. The poor Chief of the General Staff! He is summoned by the sovereign. He explains what happened. But since the sovereign's daughter is there playing with her doll the explanation has to be given in bowdlerized form: The strapping young ski instructor . . . The St. Wolfgang System . . . The initiation of the turn . . . The forward-downhill leaning of the body . . . The well-bent knees! . . . The well-bent knees and the pivot of the body! . . . The St. Wolfgang Stance . . . The closing of the uphill ski . . . The termination of the turn . . . The hat, the feather . . . The code is not hard to decipher. There can be no doubt the sovereign understands it. But he pretends not to. He dresses him down and dismisses him from his post. It thereby becomes clear to the former Chief of the General Staff that someone with strong pro-Serb sympathies has gotten the ear of the sovereign. And that means the Serbian threat is even more serious than he realized. But who could it be? He goes through the sovereign's inner circle. No one makes sense. He despairs. Finally one night the answer comes to him. And he cannot believe it didn't come to him sooner. How many times had he seen her play with that doll?! And he had really never realized it was wearing a sort of miniature *jelek*?! A *jelek*, he tells the editor of the *Neue Freie Presse*, a sleeveless woolen waistcoat worn by Serbian men and boys. *Jelek*, J-E-L-E-K. But Benedikt's too cowardly to print it and so are the editors of the other papers. They justify themselves by noting that the former Chief of the General Staff reeks of plum brandy. Then three physicians come to escort him to Dr. Krakauer's sanatorium. There he has plenty of time to study the map of the Balkans. And everyone there takes Serbia seriously, quite seriously . . .

That is what the satirist says. Now, Gretel: Do you suppose that the sweet, simple man understands it?

He does! He understands each and every word that comes out of the satirist's mouth! He knows exactly who everyone is and what everything means. He understands the political parts and he understands the erotic parts. And inasmuch as he laughs louder and longer than anyone else in the audience it is clear that no one understands it all as well as he does.

Afterward he hurries home to apprise his mother of that fact.

She, however, is still sound asleep. And nothing he does to her is capable of rousing her. He almost starts to wonder if she's dead. But then he slaps her hard enough that the lids of her eyes can remain shut no longer. She stares up. At an individual who is neither simple nor sweet. Mama, he says: I understand everything.

THE TOYMAKER HAS A LITTLE TREAT FOR THEM . . .

The rambunctious schoolboys halt their games when they realize that a strange old man has been watching them play.

They can't help but be disconcerted by the fixity of the old man's stare and the intensity of his breathing, by the way he is discreetly but steadily reducing the distance between them and himself, to the point that they can now make out the words he is murmuring: *Yes, oh yes, oh yes.*

On the other hand, the old man has a big smile on his face, and it is the experience of the boys that the biggest smiles indicate the friendliest intentions.

When the old man reaches them he wets his thin lips with his tongue and discloses to the boys that he is a toymaker. And with that he dispels their fears. A toymaker! Yes, a toymaker. He has only been watching them play because he has toys he wishes to give them.

The schoolboys begin to laugh and chatter because this not only explains the old man's behavior but reveals him to be an essentially benevolent figure.

Now, some boys like toys and some boys do not. Perhaps these are the kind of boys who don't?

No, he's wrong, they *do* like toys! They do! They do!

They're sure?

They're sure!

Well then, they're in luck, because he has wonderful toys for them, free toys, a free toy for each of them! And these free toys aren't far from here! The old man beckons them with a crooked finger. Follow me, boys!

One can only imagine the relief of these schoolboys, who, having feared the worst just moments ago, even that their innocence might be snatched from them, are now each on the verge of receiving a toy.

And actually this stands to reason, for it is Christmastime, the time of year when the grown-up world sets aside its ordinary concerns and conspires only to make children happy.

So the schoolboys follow the strange old man into the Christmas market, past jumping jacks and gingerbread men, past marionettes and vats of mulled wine, past fragrant fir trees and jolly brass bands, and out the other side, into the silent empty streets beyond. This way, boys! This way to the free toys! And he tells them that he harbors a secret conviction about what is in the heart of a child that puts him at odds with the rest of mankind; that sometimes doubts creep in and try to tell him he is wrong; but that every time he sees children at play he is reminded again that he is right.

They turn this way and that, the streets grow darker, it is just a bit farther to his toys. He can't wait to see the boys' faces when they set eyes on his toys!

He leads them into an unlit alleyway, because it is in this unlit alleyway that the toys are.

The toys are at the far end of the unlit alleyway.

Now behold, boys: My toys!

But the schoolboys don't see any toys. Where? What toys? Those aren't toys! And in a fury the boys turn on the old man and beat him to death.

Because probably they'd been expecting to receive the latest mechanical gizmos, windup battleships, model trains with real working steam engines, not these simple wooden figures the old man had turned on his own lathe.

They topple the old man's cart and send his wooden figures flying. Only one boy bothers to pick one up and put it in his pocket. Then they return to their games.

But their games no longer entertain them. Their toys no longer interest them.

If they spoke to someone like Dr. Krakauer, a world-renowned specialist on the psyche, he could tell them the reason why: It's because they murdered the old man. *When you murder someone . . .* And he'd go on to explain the effect of that on their psyches. *You see, murdering . . .* And he'd have something profound to say about it. But not everyone is lucky enough to be in the custody of such a clever man! Even in a city celebrated for its psychological profundities, most people still have to come up with their own reasons for why they act and feel the way they do. And the reason the boys come up with is: We are growing up!

Yes, they begin to think of themselves as big boys. They drink beer and smoke cigarettes and profess a passion for the theater. They make indecent remarks to waitresses and chambermaids and even get up to indecent things with them.

They think: This is natural. This is what big boys do.

By that logic it becomes possible to imagine that they lost their innocence in the usual way, the same way as everyone else: simply by attaining a certain age. Upon attaining this age they became subject to urges: that's all. These urges are natural and therefore have nothing to do with the beating death of the toymaker who'd gifted them toys that were not to their taste.

Of course, to sustain the illusion that their childhoods ended organically, with the passing of the years, it is necessary never to refer to the Christmastime in question. Never to mention the toymaker, or his claim to know what they longed for in their hearts. Or the fury that overtook them when they realized he did not.

Anything can be forgotten if it is never spoken of. So it is with this incident. The memory lingers on only in one of them, and only in the form of a faint unaccountable feeling that his urges have their origins in something unnatural.

This young man reads Kant and listens to Beethoven and decides one morning to live in a morally unimpeachable manner.

That day he does not take one sip of beer or drag of a cigarette. He is able to go the entire day without saying a single word to a woman. In this way he brings his life into alignment with his principles.

That night he has the chaste and cheerful dreams of a holy man or eunuch. But he wakes from these dreams to find the abovementioned incident restored to him in such vivid detail that the intervening years may as well not have happened. The young man lies trembling in his bed, and at dawn he rises in the knowledge that he is a murderer.

It is not possible to live unimpeachably so long as such a crime has not been reckoned with. He therefore reconvenes his boyhood friends, whom time and the normal processes of maturation have drawn apart from one another and dispersed across the various precincts of the city. When, however, they gather at their old stomping grounds, in the square where they used to play their games, the young man realizes that all of the others actually remain close friends, it is only he who has been drawn apart and dispersed. They sit facing him in their black frock coats, promising young lawyers and bureaucrats, each with his own family and a great deal to lose. So what happens next is practically preordained. They close ranks against him. They shut him down. Who? What toymaker? What on earth are you talking about? Have you lost your mind? And so forth. Even when he licks his lips and puts on a big smile and beckons the others with a crooked finger—*Follow me, boys!*—they claim not to know what he is referring to, they make a show of laughing at him, they conspire to make him feel like "an odd duck!" They accuse him of being subject to urges far more powerful and perverse than those he claims to have transcended, and to have shown signs of these urges as far back as they can remember, certainly as far back as the days he now describes as innocent. He's no saint, he is "one odd duck!" The men in their frock coats all get to their feet. In leaving they speak like psychiatrists: Their former companion dwells in a fantastical boyhood of his own imagining. Who knows why? But it makes them sad! He would do well to leave this invention behind and move resolutely into manhood, reality, the present. This threat is delivered in a tone of solicitude. They even pat him on the back, as if out of pity.

It is all very effective. The young man returns home in despair. He must have concocted the myth of the toymaker to avoid the conclusion that his urges are inscribed in his cells. And if they are inscribed in his cells, they cannot be overcome, only obliterated. He therefore shoots himself in the heart.

The grief-stricken father knows that the papers he discovers on his son's desk must be important, even if he himself, a mere dealer on the stock exchange, can't make heads or tails of them. So, under the misapprehension that his son stayed close his whole life to his childhood friends, the father entrusts them with his papers, along with what few things the young man possessed.

The manuscript—attributed to "Egerer, murderer-Messiah!" and containing a "theory of the female" interspersed with poems in which brothers and sisters walk hand in hand in the gloaming—is fed right away to the flames. But among the possessions they find a wooden candleholder in the shape of an angel; and the instant they set eyes on it they remember that the old toymaker, far from being a figment of their ex-schoolmate's imagination, really existed, even if they'd hardly touched him. And this is the toy he thought they would like.

Odder still: They do like it! They like it *now*. Its affectation of childlike simplicity evokes an innocence every grown-up yearns for even if they never actually possessed it. No child would like this toy. But every grown-up, harking back to his own childhood, will imagine he would have liked it. And since it is grown-ups who do the toy buying, not children, that gives this pseudo-primitive plaything great potential in the market.

They pitch it to the grief-stricken father. He happens to feel that both his son and his daughter grew up too fast, so he takes to the idea and fronts them the money. They establish Egerer's Toys—you used to peruse that colorful catalog with such solemnity!—and mass-produce the wooden figures so as to look hand-carved by some miller in the hinterland. And indeed, they fly off the shelves.

Yes, wherever there's a bourgeois child, there you will find one. And even where there's not. Your mother kept hers on the mantel, one for each year you'd been gone. At Christmastime candles burned in them. There were dolls under the tree. As if at any moment you would walk through the door and begin to play. A tragic scene. Your mother and the Maestro scarcely saying a word, let alone singing. She must have thought: I chose my art over my child, and in consequence I have neither! . . . Then one year, as I pass by their window, I see that everything has changed. No candles gutter in the twelve figures on the mantel, there are no dolls beneath the tree. Perched on the Maestro's lap, your mother is reading and rereading a letter from which she is draw-ing evident delight. How interesting, I think, that she should be so happy, in the continued absence of her daughter. Then she reads the letter aloud, and I learn the cause of her happiness—

But that is a tale for another day! Tomorrow! The tale of the mother who lost her daughter but was happy nevertheless! For now, my dear Gretel, I kiss you good night!

V

THE UNDERSTUDY USURPS THE ROLE . . .

Your mother, the amateur mezzo-soprano, has been named third understudy to the lead role in the operetta *Manuela la Molinera* (Manuela the Miller's Wife).

Her second husband, the well-connected singing teacher, must have called in this favor because he had failed by ordinary marital means to make her happy.

But if *this* makes her happy, it can only be due to her considerable theatrical naivete. For no fewer than three women stand between her and the stage, the first two understudies and the principal actress, all of whom would have to fall ill at the same time before your mother would be called upon to play Manuela.

And how likely is that?

Now, the part, as it happens, was composed for someone else altogether. It was intended for Klamt, the aging starlet. But Klamt, as you'll recall, has for many years been confined to the Sanatorium Dr. Krakauer because she refuses to concede that the General Intendant's daughter, now deceased, once spoke the words *Your name is Bohuslav, you are a bricklayer.*

Will she not concede that even for a starring role?

No!

That is how little the theater now means to her!

All she wants now is a child, because the love of one's child, to her present way of thinking, is worth more than the acclaim of strangers.

One day Silberberg, the venerable actor and tenor, pays her a visit. He has been cast as the miller Alfonso, but they say the operetta won't go forward unless Klamt agrees to play the wife. Will she reconsider?

She will not.

Speak loudly, please.

She won't!

Ah, that's a shame, the composer and librettist will be sorry to hear it. However, there is another little matter he wishes to discuss . . .

Silberberg has begun to fear that the public regards him as old. The monstrous hall of the New City Theater taxes his lungs and swallows his voice. He is regarded as a vestige of the old theater, of the prior century. He can see it in his ambitious understudy's impudent stare, hear it in the laughter elicited at his expense. Whenever he puts his ear trumpet in his ear to hear precisely what's so comical, the young people either change the subject or speak in a kind of young person's code—"Lighting in the theater is not merely a means of letting the audience see the stage . . ." And the young people laugh. So then, they think he's old! That he's got one foot in the grave! He grew intent on giving the world proof of his continued vitality. But how? He brooded on the problem, and finally hit upon the stratagem of marrying a woman half his age and having by her a child. What's more, he'll appear beside this wife and child wearing footwear and apparel that reflect the latest fashions. Lastly, he will apply to his skin various rouges and unguents and don a wig so subtle everyone will simply assume the hair's growing straight out of his own head. So! That is the stratagem. Will she take part in it?

He inserts his ear trumpet and angles the opening toward her mouth.

This is not the marriage proposal Klamt had dreamed of as a little girl. But it serves her present purposes. She no longer requires romance, all she wants is a child. In exchange for that she is happy to serve as an octogenarian's prop. And if he regards the child as a prop, all the better! After years competing for the adoration of the crowd Klamt will be happy to have her child to herself.

He takes her hand. Will she take part in the stratagem?

Yes, she will.

Speak loudly, please, and into the trumpet.

She will!

They proceed forthwith to Dr. Krakauer's office. It is possible, Klamt concedes, that the General Intendant's daughter said the words *Your name is Bohuslav, you are a bricklayer*. She thereby demonstrates her sanity and obtains her freedom.

When their daughter is born, Silberberg primps himself, puts the girl in a pram and Klamt at his side, and ambles like that down the main promenade.

All those who had written him off as a vestige of another era cannot but be confounded to see him strolling through the city with his young bride and even younger baby, in his absolutely contemporary shirt, shoes, and trousers!

He cannot hear what everyone is whispering as he passes because he wouldn't dare use his ear trumpet in public, but having portrayed the common man onstage many times he can well imagine what the whispers consist of. A child! At his age! Commendable . . . Is that his own hair? . . . I'm not sure, but I think so . . . I think so, too . . . And I think so, too . . . His shirt is very "of the moment"! Commendable . . . His trousers are current and his wife is young . . . That is hardly a man who will cede the stage anytime soon! . . . His poor understudy! . . . Indeed! . . .

In the privacy of their home Silberberg retires to his room and doesn't say another word to Klamt or their daughter until the following week's walk.

And that suits Klamt perfectly. She puts the crib beside her bed and delights in the rigors of motherhood. Motherhood alone is quite sufficient! Certainly she does not need *Manuela la Molinera*, whose composer and librettist beg her in vain to take the part. The sad exertions of the half-senile old stage star show her how right she was to trade the acclaim of the crowd for the love of one's child.

She has her daughter and her daughter has her. They need no one else.

Of course it is not as though the little girl does not notice the strange old man who huffs and puffs around the apartment reeking of ointment and readjusting his wig. In her picture books she lingers longest on the faces of men. Surely the girl's father has not long to live; is it cruel to her to keep her from him?

At the very least Klamt doesn't want her daughter years hence to have grounds to accuse her of that.

So one day she brings the little girl into Silberberg's room and puts her on his lap: She is yours, after all! You might as well say something to her.

At first Silberberg is confused, because the stratagem has been successful even without this. But then he realizes this has got nothing to do with the stratagem, it's got to do with some womanish emotion or other.

And what should he say to her?

Anything! Tell her something, anything, let her hear your voice.

He tells her about life, what the heart has to do moment by moment simply to sustain the human organism, and death, how our blood pools at our lowest point when at last the heart ceases to beat. But she's not interested in that. So he tells her about the history of the

French theater in its finest century, the nineteenth—Labiche, Augier, Meilhac, Hugo, Coquelin *père et fils*. But she is not interested in that, either. Then is there nothing she's interested in?! It always astonishes him how incurious are the young people of today, he tells Klamt as she snatches back her now wailing baby.

There, there, Mama has you . . .

Well, she tried! Klamt cannot be accused of keeping her from him.

There, there. But even back in their room she won't stop crying. He doesn't mean to be mean, he is just very old, it's been a long time since he was a child! We won't do that again, I promise!

Nothing consoles her. Never has Klamt seen a tantrum like this. The girl shrieks and thrashes, she hurls her toys at the wall. Is she ill? Possessed? Call a doctor! But Silberberg won't do that. Doctors cannot even tell the dead from the living, every day living persons are placed in coffins and buried in the earth, that is a documented fact. No, no—no doctors. Let me have a look at her.

You've done enough! Please go away! She is scared of you!

He barges in.

The little girl stops crying.

And when he picks her up, she smiles.

There, you see, she just wanted her father. You were upset Mama took you away, is that all it is? Come, come, no need for tears! I shall tell you about Labiche, Augier, Meilhac, Hugo, and the two Coquelins . . .

And off they go to Silberberg's room.

So it turns out the child is stupid. And if a child is stupid then it isn't the case that her love is worth more than the acclaim of strangers. It's actually the other way around, the acclaim is worth more than the love. Because the stupid child's love is given out willy-nilly, whereas the acclaim of strangers must be earned.

Klamt informs the management of the New City Theater, which had finally put *Manuela la Molinera* into production without her, that she will, after all, play the lead.

Now think what that means for your mother, my dear Gretel! The former principal is demoted to the first understudy; the first becomes the second; the second the third; and the third understudy is now the *fourth* understudy. The fourth understudy! Four women now stand between your mother and the stage! True, one of them used to be mad, but now she can safely be said to be sane. And the other three have never for an instant departed from reason, they are sturdy individuals with robust constitutions. Yet your mother still imagines she might make it to the stage? That four women, three of them sturdy, will fall ill simultaneously?! The zeal with which she rehearses the part therefore earns her the scorn of the other Manuelas.

If only (they tell her) she were more like Silberberg's understudy! Now there is someone who has extinguished his ego . . .

It's true. As a boy he saw Silberberg play Faust and decided then and there to be an actor. But his highest ambition was to serve as Silberberg's understudy, since Silberberg had brought the art of acting to a state of perfection. One could serve the theater best by serving Silberberg. And now he is doing just that. He wants nothing more. Except that it would be nice, perhaps, if Silberberg spoke to him. Even just once, even just one word. For now he contents himself with standing on the great man's marks and touching the props he's touched. He stares at him from the wings, because actors want to be watched and by staring at them one communicates something of one's devotion to them.

Then one day, the week of the premiere, the understudy puts his hand in his coat pocket and finds Silberberg's calling card.

His hand trembles as he deciphers the note scrawled on the back.

The honor of his company is requested at eight o'clock that night!

Naturally the understudy, who has been preparing for just this summons from the time he was a boy, already knows what he will tell Silberberg. He'll tell him what it meant to him to stumble on Silberberg's genius as an unworldly youngster, the son of a poor pious sacristan who, every Sunday, as soon as the church doors closed behind the last parishioner, used to—et cetera. But when he arrives at eight o'clock sharp, with a bottle of fancy cognac in hand, Silberberg is already snoring in some distant room. And to the question of whether he should not be awoken, Klamt replies: No. The very old, like the very young, need their sleep. In saying so she gestures at her daughter, even though the little girl appears to be wide awake and staring at the understudy between the slats of her crib. Hello, he says. What's your name? But she doesn't respond. Klamt laughs. I take it you do not have children! No, she can't understand yet. I became a mother too young, don't you think? She uncorks the understudy's cognac, pours two glasses, and proceeds to seduce him, because her husband's advanced age means that he can't satisfy those urges to which women, too, are subject. At first he is appalled: Your husband! Your daughter! The old man is asleep for the night, and this one, as I say, understands nothing. You are cute, little one, but what do you understand? The understudy fends her off but becomes drunk for the first time in his life, and as he grows drunk he begins to tremble with rage. So, Silberberg could not even bother to stay awake until eight?! Will he never say so much as a single word to him?! Then he will have to be satisfied with standing where the great man has stood, and touching what he has touched. He's really asleep? He's really asleep! You're sure? I'm positive. Then the understudy succumbs to her advances.

Afterward, as he buttons his trousers, her daughter, whose crib he suddenly realizes she has long since outgrown, startles him by speaking: Mama?

Yes, little one?

Mama, did you know that on his first tour of America, in 1888, Coquelin the Elder performed *Les Précieuses ridicules* before Mrs. Cleveland, the wife of the American president? His reception is said to have been *most* cordial. Naturally he played the part of Mascarille.

I didn't know that, little one, how fascinating, says Klamt, glancing at the understudy with an expression of tedium. And then, by way of explanation, Klamt adds: Oh, she knows a great deal of trivia about the history of the French theater in the century before our own, but I hardly consider that "understanding," do you? Understanding occurs in the heart. Otherwise we should have to say that Gautier's *Histoire de l'art dramatique en France* possesses "understanding"!

Mama, Emperor Napoleon III presented Sarah Bernhardt with a diamond brooch for her performance of the troubadour Zanetto in François Coppée's *Le Passant*, did you know that?

I did not, replies Klamt, adding sotto voce to the understudy: I don't call that "understanding."

He staggers out the door and into the streets. It is well known that Silberberg keeps a pistol in his dressing room. He would be within his rights to shoot the understudy dead. Therefore the next morning the understudy boards a train heading to the province of his birth. But when the train begins to move he jumps off and runs to the theater. He will let Silberberg shoot him in the head, and in that way he will serve the theater. He even imagines that Silberberg might say something to him before shooting him, even if only one word . . .

But he arrives to find the theater in a tumult. They had been rehearsing the last scene, in which Manuela and the miller, reunited, dance a fandango to celebrate their happiness, while the miller sings, fortissimo, the song "I found her in the shade of the green olive tree . . ." when Silberberg's heart had failed him. He had collapsed in Klamt's arms. He is dead. The understudy receives loud condolences and whispered congratulations. He will play Alfonso the miller. There are so many ways to serve the theater! He thought he would serve it in one way, but now he must accustom himself to serving it in a different way.

That is the first surprise. The second is Silberberg's will, which dwells principally on his fear of premature burial, and charges his wife, child, and understudy with the following task: *After the funeral ceremony, my corpse is not to be buried straightaway but rather taken to the cemetery morgue and placed in an open coffin, where for no fewer than two days—in full—it is to be observed closely and continuously for signs of life by my designated representatives (and not only by doctors, whose negligence is infamous).*

So for a second time the understudy finds himself in a room with Silberberg's wife and daughter. Only this time it's the morgue, and he's dressed as the miller Alfonso. Normally one wouldn't want to attend a funeral like that, in a traditional Andalusian vest and hat, let alone a vest and hat that belonged to the dead. But he has no choice, he'll have to go directly from the morgue to the premiere. So what if tongues wagged at the ceremony? He is not here to observe etiquette, he is here to serve the theater.

He prefers to serve the theater this way, actually. One needn't get shot in the head to make a small contribution to the theater! The hat fits him, the vest fits him, he's thirty-nine years old, he is ready to be an actor! The spell is broken. He's ready to be an actor.

Were it not for the sorrow of Silberberg's daughter he would feel almost glad the old man is dead.

For hours she stares at her father's corpse in its coffin. Yet the longer she stares at it, the less sad she seems. Is that a smile on her lips? Then suddenly she turns to the understudy and grins. It's a trick, you know! Papa is tricking you! It's a trick, Mama, did you know that?

She writhes free of the arm her mother has draped around her shoulders and squeals: He is tricking you!

At first the pathos of the little girl's delusion breaks the understudy's heart. In time, though, he realizes that she's right: Silberberg's chest is going up and down. Just a little bit, but enough. It's his greatest role. By playing a corpse for forty-eight hours he will prove his vitality to the world and give his understudy his comeuppance.

The understudy tears off the hat and the vest and prostrates himself on the floor of the morgue.

But Klamt only laughs. She smooths her big ruffled Andalusian skirt. Why do children always think they understand everything better than everyone else, when in fact they understand nothing? It is quite normal for muscles to spasm after death, for gases to escape. I know it is scary but these are natural things the body does when it dies.

And the doctor agrees, this is natural. Even when, at the forty-eight-hour mark, Silberberg's body sits bolt upright, turns to the understudy, and speaks—"Aha! Aha!"—the distinguished physician chalks it up to nature, lays the body back down, nails the coffin shut, and has it buried in the earth.

As the dirt hits the wood the girl wails and grips her mother.

There, there, little one, take your time, the theater can wait!

And, indeed, the time printed on the tickets comes and goes. An hour passes, an hour and a half. Still the curtain doesn't rise. Klamt will come! She'll come, they know it! They've already had to announce an understudy for the miller, they are loath to announce one for the miller's wife, too. To pass the time, the Duke takes his youngest daughter backstage to greet the actors. The understudies for Manuela gather around the delighted little Princess to lavish praise on her pretty dress and doll. You were just about that age the last time your mother saw you, but one wonders whether that even occurs to her. All of a sudden Klamt barrels through. *Pardonnez-moi!* Your mother is cast out of the circle as Klamt, radiant in the knowledge that she need not sacrifice the crowd for her child, or her child for the crowd, that both can love her at once, kneels before the Princess and holds out her hand for the doll. May I see? Is it a boy or a girl? What an interesting outfit! Although—

It is then that the Pan-Slavist obstetrician's bomb goes off.

Klamt and the first three understudies are among those who bear the brunt of it. Your mother, just behind them, is unscathed. Even as she attends to the dying and the dead, and the city turns its attention to war, it cannot escape her that she is now due to make her debut at the New City Theater.

I am Manuela! she must think. I am Manuela *la Molinera*!

V

THE VETERAN HEARS A VOICE AS HE STANDS IN LINE FOR
VEGETABLES . . .

Hello there, handsome!

Who? Him?

Yes, him!

It's a woman speaking. A very small but very beautiful woman
perched on the knee of a gentleman in black. She lifts her two
slender arms and points her ten fine fingers at the veteran to show
that it is really him she is addressing.

Come over here and give us a kiss, soldier!

She can't really want to kiss him, not with his face like it
is. She must be making fun of him. And anyway, he's not
supposed to step out of line because if he does he'll have
to go to the back, and by the time he gets to the front there
will be no more vegetables to be had. He jingles the coins in
his pocket. He mustn't lose those either, or spend them on anything but vegetables. Mother needs the vegetables for vegetable
soup.

C'mon, soldier, one little kiss!

She must be making fun of him. But to his surprise, the gentleman in black takes it quite seriously. He tries everything to shut her up. First he puts a hand over her mouth. But she spits that away. Then he covers her mouth with both hands. But she manages to pry his hands loose and fling them away. He calls her a tease, a coquette, and even worse things than that.

You shouldn't call her such things, warns the veteran, taking a step toward them. And if she wants to kiss someone, that's up to her!

My hero! she cries. Come kiss me!

She means it. She would not have struggled so hard if she didn't. He shuffles toward her. Then it is only a matter of making his way through the thick throng of children by whom the pair is surrounded. That isn't hard, he forges a path with his crutch. But the children start to laugh. And the veteran realizes, Oh, it's not a real woman, it's a puppet! And the gentleman is a ventriloquist!

And now the veteran himself just has to laugh. Because that is not a bad joke, not at all! He had been made to think that the woman wanted to kiss him, when really no one did.

He tips his cap at the ventriloquist, who thanks him for his service and tells the children to clap for him. Then the veteran returns to the line. But his place has been taken. He goes to the back of the line, but by the time he gets to the front the vegetables are all gone.

He cannot go home empty-handed. His mother is very clever, she'll ask clever questions and figure out what happened. That he was lured out of line by a woman. That the woman claimed to want to kiss him, and seemed sincere in this desire. But that she turned out to be a puppet.

Fool! his mother will say.

And she'll kiss his forehead and begin to sob.

You will always be my handsome boy, she'll say. But I'm your mother! The world sees you differently now, you've got to accept that. Because of what happened to you at the Vistula.

That was back at the start of the war, when no one knew whether the little Princess would live or die and everyone fought like madmen on her behalf. He had run toward the Russians and woken up in a hospital with his head wrapped in bandages.

Until you accept that certain things are simply not in the cards for you, unscrupulous people will keep taking advantage of you! That's what his mother will say, that's what she always says. It's easy to trick someone who wants something impossible!

And now, she'll say, we have nothing for soup . . .

He can't bear to hear all that again. So he can't let her know he's been tricked. The veteran vows not to go home until he's found a nice big vegetable or two to bring home with him. Then his mother will have entirely different questions to ask him, not *What made you think she wanted to kiss you?* and *Was she real?* but *How'd you find such a wonderful vegetable?* and *How'd you find two of them?* He shuffles from market to market and stands in line after line. In doing so he passes a lot of pretty women. Because their husbands are still away at the front he knows they must be very lonely and thus hankering for the company of a man. Even so, none of them so much as look at him as he passes, they all look away from him. Well, one or two look at him, even right at his face, which he knows is not easy to do. But he can see that they're doing it out of pity, they are proud of themselves for doing it. And when a woman is proud of herself for looking at you she does not want to kiss you. At least not on the lips. He could probably make them kiss him—he is probably strong enough, even mangled as he is—but that would be wrong. Plus it would do away with the thing that must be most wonderful about a kiss, which is that the man and woman touch their lips together because they want to. They both want to do that. How wonderful! His mother is right, it won't happen to him. *She* kisses him, that's true. But that's different. Because that's his mother. And it's not on the lips, either, it's on the cheek or the forehead. There is something about the forehead that isn't the lips. His mother's right, he has to accept it, no one will ever kiss him on the lips, not of her own free will, not with a face like this. She must have known that the moment the doctors unwrapped his head. They had lied to him: It's a miracle! Barely a scratch! But his mother's expression told him the truth. He was unrecognizable, hardly human.

These are sad thoughts. At the same time as he is having them night falls and the markets close. Ordinarily with such sad thoughts he would seek the comfort of his mother. But in the whole city he hasn't found a single vegetable, and he can't go home empty-handed. It happens that he finds himself beside the canal. So he fills his pockets with rocks and steps to the edge. Then a voice addresses him from a nearby bench.

Sir? Are you all right?

Leave me alone. This has nothing to do with you.

Of course it has something to do with me! A handsome man wants to ruin my evening by committing a mortal sin! I'd rather he take the stones out of his pockets and come sit down beside me.

She shouldn't call him handsome, she can't even see him in the darkness.

You have a handsome voice, she says. Handsome voices belong to handsome men.

At that moment the streetlamps turn on. The woman does not recoil. You see? she says. I knew it. Handsome! Come sit down.

The veteran's joy knows no bounds. But it is short-lived. Because it's not only the woman who can see him, he can see her, too. She's pretty, and young, not much older than a girl. But she is perched on the knee of a gentleman in black.

It is one thing to get tricked by one ventriloquist, that can happen to anyone, but it's quite another thing to get tricked by two of them.

Please! he cries. Leave me alone! I may not be as clever as some people, but I'm no fool! I know it's not really you who's speaking, you aren't real, you're a puppet, *he's* just making you say these things.

She laughs a girlish laugh. Not real? Sir, I can assure you that I am real, and that it is I who am speaking! Watch.

The gentleman takes a long swig from a bottle of beer. While he is drinking, the young woman recites the entire alphabet with absolute clarity. The veteran is amazed. Clever or not, he knows enough to know that one cannot drink and speak at the same time.

Then the gentleman takes another swig and the woman does the alphabet again. So that is even more proof.

Then the gentleman lifts her off his knee, places her on the bench, and removes himself to a considerable distance. Then, while the gentleman remains at that distance, the woman says: Hello.

Now the veteran is truly dumbfounded. Either the gentleman is a very great conjurer, perhaps the greatest the world has ever known—or else the woman is flesh and blood.

Can it be, he murmurs, that you really are real?

I'm real, she says. Come sit with me, have you got money?

How badly he wants it to be true! But that is exactly why he is liable to be tricked. He approaches her skeptically, feeling above her head for wires or string. But there is nothing there.

You're really real, aren't you?

I'm real, I'm real, have you got money? How much money have you got?

He sits on the other end of the bench. She slides over to him. From here he can even smell her skin. It smells wonderful. She is flesh and blood. That means she's got free will. And that means she's doing the things she's doing only because she wants to do them.

Show me how much money you've got.

He shows her. She takes it.

Any more?

No.

All right, she says, lying down on the bench. Let's go.

The veteran can't help but marvel aloud at what is happening. For this is the very thing which, on account of his having a face like this, Mother said would never, ever happen.

The young woman laughs. A face like what? Come on, do you want it or not?

When, however, the veteran leans over her to kiss her on the lips, she turns her head aside and says he can do anything but that.

Now it is his turn to laugh. Anything but that?! But that's the whole point, kissing on the lips is the point! For a moment there he thought his mother was wrong, but no, she is not wrong, she's right. Of course she's right, she's always right. He has been tricked again, because what he wants is impossible.

He demands his mother's money back. But the young woman won't give it back. He explains that he is a lot stronger than her, even mangled as he is. If she won't give the money back then he'll have to take it back by force. And he has half a mind to take that kiss on the lips while he's at it. But while he's explaining all this to her and even giving her a sample of his strength the gentleman in black reappears and wallops him in the stomach, then kicks him in the teeth.

When he wakes up it is morning. His mouth hurts, the grass is wet, his crutch is gone. But not far from where he's lying a vegetable seller is setting up her stall. If he hurries he might be first in line. He crawls over and staggers to his feet. First in line! Not even a vision of the Virgin Mary could tempt him to leave it. But when the old vegetable seller asks him what he wants he sticks his hand in his pocket and remembers that his money is gone.

Now, what happens next is the part of this tale he'll tell his grandchildren when they beg him for stories from the war. The rest of it will simply drift away, because the world is good and we retain the things that show us that. The old woman looks at his uniform, looks at his face, and produces from beneath her apron a whole head of cauliflower.

My dearest Gretel, I kiss you three times—one, two, three! Good night!

W

THE WAIF WANDERS THROUGH THE WORLD . . .

And no one cares about her, because they all have problems of their own.

When she was little they used to give her scraps of food, but now that she's big they don't do that anymore. What scraps there are are given to the wounded.

If a grown-up gives her something now there is always some reason for it. They want something from her in return. And that's different from how it is for other children, those plump, happy children who, because someone loves them, receive things for no reason, and in return for nothing.

The waif wanders clear across the city without finding a morsel to eat. She comes to the edge of the woods. And since she has no one to warn her not to enter them, that is just what she does. But there's nothing to eat there either, not even one wild berry. And before long she loses her way. She walks until she can walk no farther, then lies down on the ground and waits to die. She does not mind going to Heaven, because no one here will miss her, but the fact is that death is scary, so when she hears it coming she squeezes her eyes shut and does her very best to be brave.

But it is not death that is coming, it's a puppy. First she hears its little yap, then feels the scratch of its tongue on her cheek. She opens her eyes to find an old woman kneeling beside her. You poor thing! And the waif feels herself being lifted up.

She wakes in a bed softer than she thought any bed could be. A fire crackles in the fireplace. There are paintings on the walls. A beautiful bird gazes at her from a glittering cage, the friendly pup slumbers at her feet, and the old woman sits beside her, cupping her forehead with her hand.

Good morning, my child. Your fever has come down. Now you must be famished. May I bring you some fresh milk and honey cakes?

The waif nods.

How many cakes would you like, would you like a great many?

Yes, please.

Such a polite child. The cakes are in the oven, I'll go fetch them. Please make yourself at home. Bertha here you've already met. She will accept all the affection you care to give her, and more besides. She is a sweet little thing, you needn't fear that she'd ever nip you. Karl, however, does not like to be touched. He is a clever creature but easily spooked. When I found him he was circling those trees yonder, round and round, squawking in terror, although nothing was pursuing him. Best to keep your fingers out of his cage. Now then! The honey cakes.

The old woman goes off to busy herself in the kitchen, singing all the while.

The waif pets the puppy and waves at the bird. Then she looks at the paintings. Some are big and some are small, but all of them are of children, alone or in pairs, or, in the case of one painted right on the wall, in vast numbers. How fortunate she is to have come to the home of someone so fond of children!

The old woman returns with a plate of cakes and a glass of milk.

You have pretty paintings, the waif says.

I do, don't I?

You have a pretty voice, too. The prettiest in the whole world.

Thank you, my child. But that's not true, my father's baritone was more beautiful. Now please, eat, eat!

The waif drinks the milk and devours the cakes. The old woman refills her glass and plate, and, what's even better, feels her forehead again with her hand.

How can she ever repay the old woman's kindness? She has nothing to give her.

My child, there is nothing I want from you.

The old woman tends to her all day long and tells stories at bedtime, true stories from her own life. How she was born in a tub in this very house. How her mother died when she was young. How her father raised her and her six brothers, and ran the mill all the while. How times were tough but they were always sing-ing. Then she sings the waif to sleep.

The waif wakes in sunlight with Bertha batting at her and begging to be petted. She is happy to oblige. To the beautiful bird, watch-ing from his cage, she says: I would pet you, too, if I could!

Then she tidies up her bed and sees what chores there are to be done, for by making herself useful she hopes to put off as long as possible the hour when she'll be told it is time to leave. But the old woman takes the broom from her hands and tells her that there is nothing for her to do. Drink your milk, eat your cakes, and be happy, my child. Your only task here is to eat, drink, and be happy.

She stays all that day and another night, and then another day and another night.

On the fourth day, while petting Bertha again under Karl's watch-ful eye, it occurs to her to wonder if he does not like to be touched only because he has never been touched in a friendly manner.

The old woman is out in the garden gathering herbs.

The worst that can happen is he draws a little blood.

So the waif puts her finger into the cage and gently strokes Karl's neck. The bird does not bite her; however, he speaks to her in a human voice:

I am a famous writer!

Hastily she withdraws her finger. That silences the bird. But he cocks his head and peers at her so beseechingly that she reaches into his cage and touches him again. Whereupon he says:

I am a famous writer, I am a famous writer! When the war broke out I wanted nothing more than to serve at the front because it is glorious to fight for the Fatherland and glorious to die for the Fatherland. As I have written, as I have written. So I polished my saber and buckled it to my side, and I pulled on my military boots. And I said to my daughter: Don't cry! I shall have to be brave, and so shall you. And I explained to her the nature of bravery, the nature of bravery. But she knew all about it from one of her picture books. She demonstrated how to summon one's powers of bravery, and by means of a kiss she gave half of hers to me. Don't cry, Papa, now you are brave and a half! However, I was not permitted to go to the front. Understand, not permitted. I was told that I was a cultural treasure. That I could do more for the Fatherland with words than with weapons. They put me in the Press Office. Oh, it was agony to be stuck in that villa, writing about the sacrifices of other men. Agony to be in the villa. Yet the public thought I had pulled strings to be there. Their whispers and smirks when I strolled through the city indicated as much. I wanted nothing more than to fight and even to die, but nothing could persuade them of that, not even my essays on the gloriousness of those very things. Not even the saber I still kept polished and buckled to my side. Not even my boots, not even my boots. My daughter was tormented by her schoolmates, it was in vain that she explained that I had all my own powers of bravery plus half of hers. I'm a famous writer! I'm a famous writer! Then the war began to go poorly, they needed more men, I was told I was to serve at the front as a cavalryman. How pleased I was. In my essays I had explained a hundred times why the war was good, and now I would get to go to it. To leave the villa and go to it. First I took a walk. I walked across the city and into the woods. Very pleased! Very pleased! Now I could show my daughter how right she was to call me brave. But before I could turn back to report for duty I stumbled on this little mill. Through the window I saw bookshelves filled with books, all of them mine, in every conceivable edition. It's always a pleasure to meet my readers, a pleasure to meet my readers. But when the old woman opened the door the books vanished and I realized she was a witch. She transformed me into a bird. At home they must think that I've deserted, fled, but nothing could be further from the truth, it's just that I am a bird now. You see, I wish I could have fought, but I was and am a bird. During the worst of the hostilities I had the misfortune to be a bird. It grieves me to imagine what they are telling my daughter, but none of it is true, I'm not a shirker, I'm a bird, not a coward, a bird.

Just then the waif sees the old woman coming up the walk. She draws back her finger, but before she can extract it from the cage the bird seizes it in his beak and says:

Take that poker by the fire and impale her through the heart with it. Then I shall turn back into a man, and my daughter will have her father again. And you will save yourself, too. You're a clever girl, you must know by now that the witch wants something from you, no one does such things out of the goodness of their heart.

The key turns in the lock.

The waif frees her finger, runs to the fireplace, and grabs hold of the poker.

Because the bird is right, no one does such things out of the goodness of their heart! Not to a child who isn't their own.

But as the door opens, doubts enter.

What if the bird is lying? What if it is only a bird—a tricky bird, but a bird? And even if it was a man transformed into a bird, couldn't he still be wrong about the old woman's feelings?

At the last moment the waif lowers the poker and tends to the fire with it.

Thank you, my child, but you needn't concern yourself with that, the old woman says, hurrying to take it from her. Drink the milk, eat the cakes— Oh! You're bleeding!

The old woman snatches the waif's finger and brings it to her eye.

Then, without a word, she lifts the birdcage off its hook, brings it outside, and opens its little door. At first Karl won't fly away. So she turns the cage over and bangs on it until he falls to the ground. Then he flies to a nearby tree and settles on its lowest branch.

When she comes back in she bandages the waif's finger and covers it in kisses. Forgive me! the old woman says, starting to cry. It wasn't right of me to keep such a beautiful but bad-tempered bird where it could tempt the curiosity of a child. I should have let him go the moment you arrived. Now I fear you'll want to leave. And today of all days . . .

Why today of all days?

Today I was going to ask you to stay with me forever. Listen—

And she tells another story. When her mother died, she sought comfort from her father. But his attention was divided among all seven of his children. Since her brothers were excellent singers, she contrived that each of them should be sent to a boys' choir in the city. As they left home one by one she got more and more of Father's attention, until at last she got all of it. Then she was happy. But when she grew up, and came to the city, a clever doctor got her in his clutches and convinced her it was otherwise. Her childhood wasn't happy, it was unhappy. Her father wasn't kind, but cruel. Everything that afflicted her at present was the consequence of crimes he had committed against her. At first she could not recall any of these crimes. The doctor assured her that was normal. Gradually, over the course of years, he helped her remember what had happened in that big, dark, bare house. When her father lay dying she refused to visit him, even though he wrote her letter after letter asking why not. Her suitors she chased away, too, because she knew that all of them were capable of doing to their children what her father had done to her. She wanted justice. Yet there was no way to obtain it. That was how she spent her life. But not long ago, while walking in the woods, she stumbled on her long-abandoned childhood home. It was not anything like she remembered it. It wasn't big, but small. Not dark, but light. Not bare, but filled with art. A cozy little cottage with flower-boxes in the windows. New memories came back to her, this time true memories. How her father had painted the paintings, how he had hung the flowerboxes. He had done all he could to give her a happy childhood in spite of the fact that her mother was gone. And she had let him die alone! Because of that doctor! That Dr. Krakauer! All of a sudden she wanted a child, she wanted to raise a child here, in this house. To give a child as happy a childhood as she herself had been given. But she was very old now, too old to have a child. Still, she prayed to God for one, for hadn't God given Sarah one at ninety? And God must have heard my prayers, the old woman says, because He gave me you. That's why I was going to ask you to stay. To give me the gift of watching you grow into womanhood. But why should you want to stay, she adds, tearfully kissing the waif's finger, if I can't even keep you safe here . . .

No, I do want to stay! I do! I will!

And the waif flings her arms around the old woman, who, in celebration, brings out an enormous quantity of honey cakes and fresh milk. Eat and drink, eat and drink, grow and grow and grow, my child. More cakes, more milk, grow and grow and grow.

So, the bird was half-right, but half-wrong. It is true that the old woman wants something from her. But what she wants is only the gift of watching her grow into womanhood.

And indeed, the waif grows and grows and turns into one of those plump, happy children she used to envy. And the more she grows, the more delighted the old woman becomes. Oh, my, she says, feeling the fat on the waif's bones: You are becoming a wonderful young woman! And in this way the waif learns what love is.

Of course, it is in the bird's interest to convince her otherwise. Often as she eats her cakes by the window he flutters just outside and pecks frantically at the pane. One day he finds his way down the chimney and alights on her head, giving himself the power of speech. How to persuade the poor girl that she remains unloved? That where she thinks she's found love she will find only more suffering? A challenging task even for a poet. I am, he begins, a famous writer; but before he can say another word the dog leaps into the air and walks off with the bird in her jaws.

X

THE X-RAY TECHNICIAN EXERTS HERSELF TO EXTRACT A STAY OF EXECUTION . . .

She follows the figure of Death through the Children's Hospital.

When Death comes to a stop at the foot of a child, she knows that that child will die. But when he stops at the head of a child, that child will live.

How easy it would be for the mothers of the dying to frustrate Death's intentions! They only had to pick their children up and turn them around, so that Death stood no longer at the feet but at the head.

The mothers, however, cannot see the figure of Death, so it does not occur to them to do that. The X-ray technician yearns to tell them to do it, but they cannot see her, either. And when she speaks they can't hear her. For she dwells in a supersensible realm and can no longer communicate with the living.

Once, my dear Gretel, she was as alive as you or I. And not only alive, but happy! She was pretty, painted pretty paintings, had two loving children and a brilliant husband. But then he obtained that peculiar substance from the mines of J—, and she lost everything investigating the rays it emitted. Burns and boils afflicted her fingers and scarred her face. Her daughter, who had warned her that this would happen, ceased to recognize her and died in a mental institution. After that Otto left her to devote himself to the contemplation of God. She still had her son but she did not want to bother him, he had a family of his own now. Sons are different from daughters. That is why she needed her Hilde again. So, to see her all the sooner, the technician decided to hasten her own death. She tied a rope around the crossbar of a window and the other end around her neck.

The crossbar held, but the rope snapped in two, and instead of beholding her daughter she beheld the figure of Death.

You are not quite dead, he informed her.

But she was not alive, either. She was somewhere in between. And there, in between, was where she would remain for all eternity. For it turns out that Death was affronted by the X-ray. It was not for her to expose people's bones and tell them whether they would live or die. It was for him to do that. So from now until the end of time she would watch him do it.

And it was wartime then, so there was a great deal to do. He led her to the Serbian front, the Russian front, the Italian front. In the early days she tried yelling at the dying young men: If only they turned themselves around so that Death stood at their heads, not their feet, they could save their lives and return home to their mothers! But they couldn't hear her, so all of them died.

Then the war wound down and what soldiers were left went to the city. They brought the flu with them. So they brought Death with them also. And where Death went the technician had no choice but to follow.

First to the Children's Hospital.

Then to a tenement in the slums.

And finally to the ducal residence.

They drift through the ornate facade, up three flights of stairs, and into the bedroom of the little Princess, who even four years after the blast in the theater has still not awoken from it.

In all that time her mother the Duchess has not left her side.

She sat in a chair by the bed and did whatever was necessary to keep her child alive. It was not easy. But in a way it was gratifying to be needed again. For example, the Duchess was supposed to stand in a certain spot on the floor and hold her head at a certain angle for a certain period of time. That had to be done in the middle of the night. If she didn't do it, her child would die. A voice explained all this. So she did it. And the child lived. Or she had to check every faucet in the house, because if even one of them was dripping, even a little bit, her daughter would die by morning. This, too, was explained to her by a voice, and it, too, had to be done right away, even though the instructions came to her in the middle of the night. Or she had to tap the fringe of the carpet with both big toes sixteen times, so that her child would live. Sometimes, to be sure, she quarreled with the voices. No; please; I already did that; please let me be. But they would point out how minuscule was the cost of performing even the most onerous task compared with the value of her little girl's life. And that was true. The Duchess had little to lose by performing the tasks, and possibly everything to gain. Imagine refusing to do a task and waking up in the morning to find her daughter dead! So she did all that was asked of her. But the more she did, the more was asked of her. For example, they were no longer satisfied with sixteen taps of both big toes, she had to follow that with sixteen heel taps, too. Then she had to sneak into her husband's study, search his desk for President Wilson's Fourteen Points, and cross out Point X, concerning autonomy for the subject peoples of Austria-Hungary. If she didn't do it, then her little girl would die. The tasks took her all night, so she never slept. Her six older daughters grew concerned. They summoned Dr. Krakauer. He was able to convince her that the voices she heard were the product of her own mind, which by these means gave her the illusion of control over something that was out of her hands. So whenever the voices addressed her, she was to tell them firmly that they were not real, they had no power over her, and she did not have to do anything they said.

The doctor's advice works. The voices go away. For the first time in a long while the Duchess falls asleep as she sits in the chair by the bed.

But no sooner has she fallen asleep than Death enters and stands at the foot of her child.

The X-ray technician is heartbroken to see that. She had still been alive when the bomb went off and had prayed with the rest of the city for the little Princess to live. Now she's here to watch her die. So even though she knows it won't accomplish anything, because living people cannot hear her, she tells the sleeping Duchess to wake up, pick up her daughter, and turn her around, so that her head goes where her feet are and her feet go where her head is.

The Duchess seems to stir.

That may be a coincidence.

But in case it isn't the technician kneels beside her chair and screams into her ear: Wake up, pick up your daughter, and turn her around, so that her head goes where her feet are and her feet go where her head is!

The Duchess opens her eyes, wide. But instead of rushing to save her daughter, she sits very, very still. Then she says: You aren't real. You have no power over me. I don't have to do anything you say.

That does not discourage the X-ray technician. On the contrary, it's a good sign, because it means that the Duchess can hear her. So she screams the instructions again and again, louder and louder, right into the ear of the Duchess: Pick up your daughter and turn her around, so that her head goes where her feet are and her feet go where her head is! Pick up your daughter and turn her around, so that her head goes where her feet are and her feet go where her head is!

The Duchess clutches her own head and groans. She murmurs again the words that Dr. Krakauer taught her to say. But then, probably because deep down she knows that this voice, unlike all the others, is real, she gets up from her chair, picks up her daughter, and turns her around, so that the Princess's feet lie on her pillow.

Death, whose hands had already been reaching out for the little girl, is confounded. He execrates the X-ray technician. But she is not afraid of him. He has already separated her from Hilde forever. What more can he possibly do to her? Finally he collects himself. Slowly, leisurely, taking care to betray no desperation, he drifts around the bed up to the headboard and stands once again at the Princess's feet.

Pick her up and turn her around, so that her head goes where her feet are and her feet go where her head is! Thus the technician screams into the Duchess's ear. Then, in case it is not a matter of volume, she whispers it also. Pick her up and turn her around . . .

The Duchess clutches her own head. She squeezes her head as if trying to pop it, and then hits her head with her fists. You're not real, you have no power over me, I don't have to do anything you say. Then she picks her daughter up and turns her around. And the child lives.

Yes, the child lives, so long as she pays attention to this voice. From then on she does its bidding. The voice tells her when her daughter has to be picked up and turned around, and when she has to be picked up and put back the way she was. Since these tasks have to be performed at frequent intervals all through the night, the Duchess has no time for sleep. Dr. Krakauer is called once again. But this time, because this particular voice is not only real but important to obey, his techniques for silencing it would only do harm. She does not use them.

Death does not know what to do. He can hear the masses in the streets below. Probably they have begun to make light of him. He is famous for taking away the rich and poor without distinction, but as long as the Princess lives, while millions of others die, it probably seems he has an easier time of it with the poor! So he asks the X-ray technician what will make her stop meddling. And she replies: Let me die and go to my Hilde.

Now, it happens that the dead have neither names nor memories and are indistinguishable one from another. But he doesn't tell her that. He rows her to the other shore, returns alone to the ducal residence, and stands at the feet of the little Princess.

There is no longer any voice to tell the Duchess when to turn her daughter around.

He reaches his hands into the little girl's body and takes hold of her soul.

However, since the Duchess no longer employs Dr. Krakauer's techniques for silencing them, all the old voices speak to her again. She taps the carpet sixteen times with both big toes, then sixteen times with both heels. She stands in a certain spot and looks in a certain direction. She checks all the faucets in the house.

And that confounds Death completely. Because these are all of the most powerful means of keeping him at bay. Yet these means are known only to God. So the voices guiding her must be the voices of God, Who must have been moved to intervene by the magnitude of her love. She taps the carpet with toes and heels, double-checks the faucets, and stands in the spot. Death cannot endure that. He releases the child's soul and vanishes from her room.

At that instant the little Princess sits upright in bed.

Papa!

No, Papa's in Padua signing an armistice with the Entente. But Mama is here.

Mama, says the Princess, what time does the show begin?

Y.

THE YID'S DAUGHTER WAS NO LONGER YOUNG . . .

Yet you were still my little girl, because the world was still new to you. I had kept it new for you. You held my hand tight as I unlocked the front door. And off we went. First you had trouble seeing, it was too bright, you had to squint! Then you wanted to know what everything was. You pointed at that, and that, and that. That, I said, is the home of the Duke and Duchess, whose loyal subjects we are. That is an obscene facade which stole the innocence of the youngest Princess. That is fifty-five rambunctious boys whose voices harmonize in hymns to the Lord. That is the workers being led into the streets by a classically trained dancer and her invalid father, a former ballet master and administrator of the arts. That is a wounded veteran hobbling home with a whole head of cauliflower. And that, my dear Gretel, is the New City Theater! That is your seat, and that is mine. That's the stage, where we shall see what we have come here to see. That's the pit for the musicians. That is the box for the Duke and the Duchess and their seven daughters, all of whom will be in attendance tonight. That is the curtain rising. That's a whitewashed Andalusian village. And that—yes, who is that? This one you tell me. Who *is* that? Do you know? . . . Manuela, the miller's wife, had come onstage, sweeping and singing. I did not tell you who it was because it interested me to know whether you would recognize her. Don't you know who that is, Gretel? But you did not. It was not only that your sensitive eyes weren't accustomed to such dazzling lights, or that you had to crane your neck to peer around the large

German-Austrian man sitting in front of you. You simply did not know who it was. And why should you? So I told you. That, my dear, is a mezzo-soprano. Now come along, we needn't waste the rest of our night at an operetta! We stood up. But the others in our row, having already expressed their irritation at our whispering, were hardly inclined to move their knees. They had no intention of letting us leave. Then it dawned on me that in our whole long row there was not a single Czech, Pole, Slovak, or Slovene, not a single Hungarian, Romanian, Ruthenian, or Croat. There were only German-Austrians. That was true of the entire theater. We had to leave at once. I managed to yank you out of the row and up the aisle, only to find the exits blocked by German-Austrians. I tried a different route. German-Austrians! We went down the stairs, only to meet a horde of German-Austrians coming up the other way. We turned around and ran to the top. We pushed through one door, and then another. At last we found refuge in an empty box. It was the Duke's. Then it became clear what had happened: The workers' strike had taken a revolutionary turn. The Duke's family had fled into exile. You and I were their loyal subjects no longer. As I pieced this together, you climbed into the little Princess's seat, the best in the house, from which your view of the miller's wife was completely unobstructed. So, therefore, was her view of you. She paled, pointed, shrieked, and swooned. Two thousand German-Austrians twisted around to give us nasty looks. No, we were no longer the Duke's loyal subjects! We were not even a successful singer, an unproduced playwright, and their daughter. We were Yids, Gretel, that's all. Three noisy Yids making a scene at the theater.

Good night!

Z

THE ZIONIST ZIGZAGS . . .

He welcomes the delegation of important gentlemen.

The gentlemen are here to escort him to the Jewish State, to which he himself gave birth during an evening at the theater.

And his wife will be taken there, too?

Yes, yes.

And Gretel, their daughter?

Yes. Now—

And there they will live in harmony with one another, because in the Jewish State things will be possible that were not possible here, inasmuch as everything will be simpler than it is in the city?

Indeed. Now if you please—

All of a sudden the Zionist grows suspicious of the gentlemen. He frees his arms. He zigs and zags. But they catch him again with little trouble.

Well then, gentlemen: To the Jewish State!